**AN EPIC ILLUSTRATED NOVEL
OF FANTASY
AND SCIENCE FICTION**

An epic quest. A puzzle to tantalize not only the hero of the story, but the reader at the same time. An odyssey. A sweeping game played out across a future world.

Journey across the world of 2033, from the strange ruins of a city called Ophir to the bizarre docks of Marseilles.

Enter the Quest of the Gypsy and find yourself in the middle of Ron Goulart's most seductive s.f. mystery, a tale of deception and adventure which explodes the identity of one incredible wanderer.

Meet Jackita Teal, a rogue with the timing of a spider; and the Vulture, a strange creature who holds the clues to Gypsy's memory. Then discover a strange hero, on the verge of learning the fifty-year old secret of his past.

If you like puzzles and you love science fiction, this novel is for you.

EYE OF THE VULTURE

a novel by
RON GOULART

illustrated by
ALEX NINO

edited and developed by
BYRON PREISS

A QUEST OF THE GYPSY NOVEL

published by
Jove Books/Harcourt, Brace Jovanovich
produced by
Byron Preiss Visual Publications

WEIRD HEROES VOLUME 7

Letters of comment are welcomed. Please address mail to WEIRD HEROES SEVEN c/o Byron Preiss Visual Publications, Inc. 680 Fifth Ave., New York City 10019. If you would like to see more of the Gypsy, write Editor, Jove/HBJ Books, 757 Third Avenue, New York City 10017. The next Weird Heroes, an anthology with Farmer, Moorcock, Hickman and others will be available in Nov. '77.

This book is dedicated to Norma Nino

INTRODUCTION

An epic quest. A puzzle to tantalize not only the hero of the story, but the reader at the same time. An odyssey. A sweeping game played out across a future world.

That's what Ron Goulart and I planned when we discussed a series called, *Quest of the Gypsy*. The book you hold in your hands is the second book in the Gypsy's quest, yet as any new reader will soon find out, it is an ample introduction to all that has gone before it.

Eye of the Vulture is a complete adventure set in the maddening world of 2033. You will soon meet our hero Gypsy and shortly thereafter, you will become involved in the secrets of his past. It is a *game*, you see, and there will be a slight advantage for the reader. You will be privileged to certain information which Gypsy is not. You'll see things he doesn't. It's an edge—you get the hints while Gypsy has his *abilities*. There are some special tricks up our hero's baggy sleeve and they'll put him ahead of you at times and, at others, get him in trouble. Yet the game will be constant. Who is Gypsy? Where did he come from? What is in the murky past we piece together from the clues? Who is the mysterious vulture?

If you like puzzles, his quest is a tantalizing voyage.

The gamesmakers are Ron Goulart, Alex Nino and myself. Anybody familiar with science fiction has probably read a Goulart story at one time. He's a modern Swift, an author with a sharp pen writing about our technology and society in an ironic style that is not soon forgotten. He has an eye for hypocrisy and dehumanization. Rarely has the computer age met an adversary so adept at satire, and in *Eye of the Vulture*, there's little escape from Goulart's barbs.

Much of this *Quest* novel is set in Africa, and, just as he etched a razor sharp portrait of Europe in Book 1, now Goulart turns his typewriter to the emerging continent. Don't be surprised when Africa is not the place you'd expect it to be fifty years from now. In Gypsy's—and Goulart's—future, few places are.

Those sensitive to the current state of turmoil in Africa—and other contemporary issues—such as pornography, technology, and civil disorder—are urged to keep in mind that Goulart is a satirist and the environments he sets up for our hero are sendups of our modern stereotypes and foibles in a satirical, no-holds-barred fashion. He's likely to offend you, shake you up. There's a method to Ron's madness. By showing how things *are* in a world that doesn't exist, he's dealing sharply with what *shouldn't be* now.

The longer I know Alex Nino, the more I respect his work. Alex, who's illustrated Gypsy from the start, is a remarkable Filipino artist with more styles than Picasso—and all of them worth viewing. In addition to his recently released portfolios and posters, he has done covers for D.A.W. books and many graphic stories. "Nightmare," a 10-page black and white job, has recently appeared in the prestigious French magazine, "Metal Hurlant". Alex brings to Gypsy a sense of humor which complements Ron's nicely. He also brings his amazing brushwork and compositions, which, with the help of craftint paper, now takes on a new dimension. Lovers of fantasy art should find the fifteen or so plates by Alex to be a delight. Collectors interested in purchasing any of the originals can write us here.

Enough chatter. A quest awaits you.

Byron Preiss, Editor

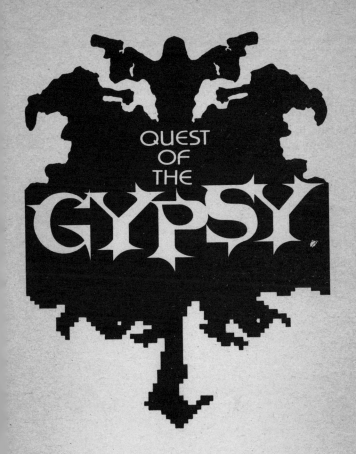

QUEST
OF
THE
GYPSY

EYE OF

THE VULTURE

The dogs delayed him.

He had been coming downhill through the misty ruins, a tall, wide-shouldered young man with his right arm in a sling of bright scarlet cloth. It was early morning and Gypsy was making for the harbor area of Marseilles Nouveau, where people still lived and business, much of it shady, was carried on.

The mist was thick and abrasive, drifting around the mounds of brick and rock, the tumbles of splintered wood, and the jagged piles of glass shards and twisted metal which had once been houses and cottages. Chunks of walls still stood, smudged with blackish mildew, and the heavy mist swirled through window holes and the remains of doorways. The roadway was muddy, rutted with pools of scummy water. You could smell the sea here, though not as strong as the odors of decaying waste.

Gypsy heard the dogs before he saw them. Up ahead of him, hidden in the morning fog, they growled and snarled, yipping at each other. At least a half-dozen of them.

He spotted the arm first, and it made him clutch at his own injured limb. The arm was, he saw as he went closer, attached to the sprawled body of a young boy. A thin, gaunt boy, not more than ten years old.

The boy was dead, the dogs were eating him. Snarling, tearing the flesh from his ribs, fighting as they did. Bloody-mawed, five of them, wild dogs, big and savage.

Gypsy had seen many of them in this part of France. "Leave him alone," he ordered, his voice deep and angry.

It really didn't make any difference. The black-haired boy was dead. But Gypsy didn't want them worrying the body that way, ripping at it with those yellow teeth.

"Get away, back!" He scooped a rock off the ground, heaved it.

A dog yelped, his attention caught.

"Back away. Get going," suggested Gypsy. He tossed another rock, which conked a second scavenging hound.

The two he had hit watched him, the other three went on eating.

The two, neck hair bristling, teeth revealed, stiff-legged, came stalking in his direction.

With a brief warning snarl one of the wild dogs leaped. It hit Gypsy in the chest, teeth snapping and then sinking into the already injured right arm. Shreds of flesh were torn away, squills of wire, twists of plastic tubing.

Without even being fully aware he was doing it, Gypsy used one of his special talents.

The air produced a faint corn-popping sound, the dog was no longer there.

In fact, all five of them had vanished.

Readjusting his scarlet sling, Gypsy ran forward to the ripped and torn body of the dead boy. His insides were leaking out of the jagged holes made by the pack of wild dogs.

"Have to bury him," Gypsy decided.

"What a ralfing stupid thing to do."

Straightening, Gypsy glanced around. The voice had been that of a young girl, but he didn't as yet see her. "Do you know who this boy is?" he asked the fog.

"Of course I do. It's only Jean-Paul."

Gypsy noticed her now, perched on the remains of a church wall. She was about eleven, long-legged and blonde, dressed in a very faded and much-frayed shift. One leg swung back and forth. Near her resting elbow, part of a stained glass window was still in place. It showed the feet and legs of a forgotten saint.

"Did the dogs kill him?" Gypsy asked.

"Of course they didn't. What a ralfing stupid question. My name is Susanne."

"I'm Gypsy. How did he die, then?"

Susanne shrugged her bare, dirty shoulders. "Around here there are always plenty of reasons," she replied. "Myself, I'd bet it was starvation. Most of the others in my group favor the Spanish influenza as the cause." Another shrug. "Who cares? The important point, Gypsy, is you've mucked up our plans."

"Letting the dogs eat Jean-Paul, that's part of a plan?"

"You don't live here in the outskirts of Marseilles Nouveau," the lean girl said. "You're merely passing through. Also, you are full-grown. We, my group and a lot of others, we live here all the ralfing time. We have to worry about the wild dogs continuously."

"You meant the body as a *peace offering*?"

"Naw, they're too rotten and nasty for that," explained Susanne, leg still swinging. "We were using him as a decoy. Keep some of them busy, while the rest of the group went food hunting. Poor Jean-Paul only managed to decoy a piddle of dogs, though. We have to contend with more than a hundred of the beasts."

"Did Jean-Paul have any family?"

The girl laughed. "People don't have families anymore."

"Some do."

"You must come from a long way off," she said. "How'd you make the dogs disappear like that?"

"It's . . ." he answered, "a thing I can do."

"Where'd they go?"

"Away from here."

Susanne, scratching at a red place on her ankle, said, "I suppose you're not so ralfing stupid at that, Gypsy. I thought you were fouling up our decoy. If you got rid of those dogs on a more or less permanent basis, that's not half-bad of you."

He nodded at the dead boy. "Now I'll bury him."

"No need. Nobody cares," she said. "Jean-Paul was

not that well liked, which may explain why he died of starvation."

Gypsy said, "I'll bury him here, in the churchyard."

"This hasn't been sacred ground for a long time," the girl said, laughing once more.

The mist cleared as Gypsy walked along the dockside street. He noticed the banners strung above him. *Welcome Smugglers! Marseilles Nouveau Greets All Smugglers! Welcome Smugglers!*

"Nope!" Gypsy's left hand swung out, clamped the wrist of the rusty chrome-plated robot which had been attempting to pick his pocket.

"Ah, forgive me, sir," the battered old mechanism told him. "I'm an honest servo basically, but, alas, I've been programmed to lead a rogue's life."

"You should ask them to oil you more often," Gypsy advised. "Your elbow squeaks."

"Once a servant of quality folks, now an unsuccessful dip," the robot sighed. "The twenty-first century, sir, has not been kind to me. Back thirty years ago, in 1997, I—"

"This is 2033—1997 was thirty-*six* years ago."

"Ah, so they've let my chronometers fall into disrepair, too." The robot shook his head, producing a new and different creak. "I appreciate your interest in my sorry fate, sir. May I be of any assistance to you?"

"I'm looking for the shop of a man named Balzac."

"A great novelist, sir. His depiction of the lives of courtesans, for instance, moved me to tears. And when you can make a robot—"

"This is a different Balzac. He runs a repair shop."

Pung!

The robot had given himself a nudge in the head with

the heel of his hand. "Time is out of joint again," he said sadly. "They've let my memory banks get out of whack."

On their left was a sidewalk café. The seven outdoor tables were occupied by naked patrons.

"What's this place?" Gypsy asked.

"Pay it no mind, sir. A low dive, catering to nudists and similarly depraved types. Imagine going around without a stitch and not even bothering to have yourself chromed. This next bistro we're passing is even more bizarre, as the name will no doubt hint to you."

"Sado-Masochist Café," Gypsy read off the sign above the green door. "Most Offensive and Brutal Waiters in the Known World."

"Things keep changing for the worse," observed the robot. "A theory, I believe, first suggested by a fellow named Spengler. He's dead by now, too, I imagine."

"So I hear," said Gypsy. "Hey, there's the shop I want, across the way there!"

"Here you go, matey! Latest catalogue! Profusely illustrated!" A Black man in a thick overcoat was roaming the sidewalk handing out glossy pamphlets. "Cast an eye on the newest arrivals at Madame Potpourri's Establishment on the fabled and nearby Riviera."

Absently Gypsy let the fellow put a pamphlet in his good hand. "Here's Balzac's," he said to the robot, "so I'll—"

"I've appreciated our little chitchat, sir. I've half a mind to try having myself reprogrammed, possibly into something clerical. I've often thought I'd look quite handsome enameled black."

"Good luck. Try not . . ." Gypsy stopped speaking.

"Something amiss, sir? You turned quite pale after casting your eye on that bordello leaflet."

"No, nothing." He thrust the pamphlet into a pocket, crossed the street, and entered Balzac's shop.

Gypsy had recognized one of the girls pictured in the handout. As soon as he had finished here, there'd be a change in his plans. He had to visit the Riviera.

"Who are you?"

"My name is Gypsy."

"But . . . who are you?"

"That I can't answer . . . not yet. I figured you might be able to help me find out."

Balzac was a large, chubby man, dark, two or three days behind in his shaving. "I'm not equipped to delve," he said. "You're much too complicated a . . . person."

Leaning forward in his wooden chair, Gypsy said, "You're not sure I'm human. You think I could be an android, a robot made to look like a human."

"If you are, you're the best one ever built." Balzac tilted back in his chair, resting his plump fingers on the workbench in his backroom studio. His fingertips played over the array of tools. "But surely, my friend, you must know about yourself."

Gypsy was watching his injured arm, which he held resting on the worktable. It was not a flesh-and-bone arm. It was made of metal, plastic, and wires. The flesh over most of it was not real flesh, and it had been torn and shredded, revealing the mechanism beneath. "You can repair my arm?"

"Yes, my friend, that much I can accomplish. Balzac has the equipment for that sort of a job. Balzac may not be Wondersmith, but Balzac is still a craftsman."

"*Wondersmith*? Who's he?"

"A brilliant man who lives out on the island of Corsica. Fortunately for him, the government of the island is relatively tolerant." Balzac picked up a small needle-pointed drill. "His workshop dwarfs Balzac's, he owns the best equipment in this part of our sorry world. He even has an X-ray machine, my friend."

"That would help," Gypsy said.

The repairman was squinting, studying Gypsy's arm. "I won't quite be able to duplicate this pseudoflesh of yours," he told him. "Very good stuff, it is, better than anything I've ever come across. The few 'bots and andies I get a chance to work on are relics of forty or fifty years ago, most of them."

"So am I."

"Difficult to accept," said Balzac. "No one had advanced that far back then, before our world had fallen apart and fragmented. Even today, in the regions of the world which have made the most progress back toward some sort of technological civilization. . . . You don't know who or what you are? Yet you are able to inform me that you're from the world of a half-century ago."

"Some things about myself I remember," Gypsy said. "Others I found out since I awakened."

"Awakened?" Balzac left his chair to shuffle to a large wooden cabinet across the room.

"Somehow, for some reason, I . . . I was asleep for those fifty years. I woke up a few weeks ago, in Paris."

"Ah, Paris," said Balzac. "Still a city filled with romance and intrigue, is it not?"

"It was full of nasty little robots the day I was there."

"A pity, a pity." He took a metal box from a high shelf in the open cabinet. "Nothing remains the same, not even romance."

"Speaking of which, do you know anything about a place called Madame Potpourri's Establishment? It's on the Riviera."

"Don't go there, my friend!" Balzac brought the box to the worktable and opened it. "This is the best I can do in the way of synthetic flesh. I purchased several yards of it some years back from a man who built Irish house servant androids. . . . That accounts for the freckles."

Watching him unroll a few inches of the plastic skin, Gypsy said, "I have to go to Madame Potpourri's, but not as a customer. I must find someone who has ap-

parently been forced to work for them."

"Then you may not survive," warned Balzac. "Even paying customers don't always get out of there alive." He held a swatch of the freckled flesh against Gypsy's arm. "Not a perfect match. I'm sure Wondersmith will be able to do much better by you, but this should suffice until you reach him. Unless, of course, you persist in the idea of storming that bordello. If you do, you may never reach Corsica."

"I'll get there."

After setting the imitation skin aside, Balzac began probing at the inner workings of Gypsy's mechanical arm. "A most amazing bit of gadgetry, highly sophisticated. Not too sophisticated for Balzac, though it comes close." He touched Gypsy's upper arm, which was not injured. "Impressive, quite impressive."

"Wondersmith will be able to tell more?"

"He's a brilliant man, as I've told you. He even invents things on his own. Makes Balzac look like a dolt by comparison. Does that hurt?" He had thrust his probe into a twist of multicolored wires.

"No, I don't feel anything."

"This is something I can patch up, at least well enough to enable you to continue on your journey. That hurt?" Another jab, a different spot.

"Um, yes."

"Fascinating, fascinating. How, my friend, did you happen to come by this injury?"

"A disagreement," answered Gypsy, "in a place named Villedeux."

Balzac brought his head closer to his work. "Overrun with robots in Villedeux, so I've heard."

"They were."

As Balzac worked, Gypsy thought again about what had happened at Villedeux, about the people he'd met,

the people he'd helped.

What had his days been like since that morning when he had awakened in Paris, since he had discovered it was the year 2033 and he had somehow lost a great segment of his life? *Fifty years*.

That didn't make sense, really. A human being couldn't survive as he had. Or could one? Could a person be put to sleep, somehow suspended, and awakened half a century later?

Most likely he was a machine, a machine not much different than the robots he'd fought against in Villedeux that had handled the Liberating process. "No, he couldn't accept that. He knew *he* was human, not just a sophisticated mechanism. Yet where had he been "stored"? How had his body been preserved? How . . . why . . . why had *he* been selected? Who *was* he?

"I know my own nature, know what I really am."

But he didn't. Nor did he know of his quest, the intricate and only partly understood game. If he were certain of himself, he wouldn't have to pursue the clues . . . roving across what was left of the world, heading for Africa . . . for Africa and some further trouble.

"Africa may not be necessary."

Yet as he said the words, Gypsy knew that he *would* continue . . . that no matter what fortune might come his way, there would still be those nagging questions . . . and that strange shadowy vulture who appeared so often and unexpectedly. The vulture had been there in Paris that first new morning. It had been originally intended to be some sort of supervisor. A perverse kind of guardian angel.

"But why?"

There was a hell of a lot yet to be found out.

So far Gypsy had found out a few things about himself, with the help of the exuberant Walpole, recruited from

the fringes of the London underworld, and the equally
unconventional Annabelle. Gypsy had more facts, had a
few more names. Names of people who'd been involved
with him and done whatever it was that had been done to
him. Fifty years ago. They weren't alive anymore. At
least he hadn't been able to find any of them.

What he *had* found were the *clues* . . . the perplexing,
half-revealing pieces of the puzzle to his past.

His name—the name they'd apparently given
him—was Gypsy. What had happened to him was part of
something called Project #72G, involving in part a long-
defunct organization known as the European Security
Office. The project had been headed up by a woman
named Dr. Hawksworth. Sometimes Gypsy almost remembered her.

"What was the purpose?"

There came to him now and then glimpses of the past,
he'd see across those lost fifty years. See Dr. Hawksworth and the chill bright room where they'd . . . worked
on him. The images always faded too soon, leaving him
with almost nothing.

The most maddening thing of all was what the vulture
had told him—that it was a game. Something which must
be played out to the finish. A blasted game! His life—or
too much of it—was being lived as if it were an amusement—a film—something not *real*. And everyone who'd
set up the damn game was dead, or lost and old.

Yet he was still playing the game, searching to find out
who he was . . . why he was playing it in the first place.

"Not as serious as Balzac thought."

"What?"

"I was saying, my friend, your arm is not seriously injured. To fix it will be a matter of an hour or two more."

"Good," said Gypsy.

"I hope while you've been woolgathering you realized

Balzac was right when he warned you not to go against Madame Potpourri."

"There are a good many things I don't know about myself," Gypsy said, grinning. "But I do know that when I make up my mind to do something, I do it."

"Admirable," said Balzac. "Also foolish."

Several nervous old men were gathering on the twilight beach. Well-dressed, looking as affluent as anyone could in the world as it was, they whispered to each other, nudged, giggled. Some of them—there were eight of them together now and three more hobbling down across the sand to join—watched not the fading waters of the Mediterranean but the rows of buildings up beyond the long, white beach. When the lights in the various bordellos and whorehouses blossomed the group of old men chuckled, murmured, did more nudging with stiff elbows.

"You can't be with *them*."

Gypsy was walking along the sand. He slowed, halted, studied the young man who'd questioned him. "Nope, I'm on my own."

The felllow was thin, dressed in a white singlet and white shorts. On his close-cropped head he wore a white, beaked cap with a scarlet feather in its band and the letter *P* on the front. "I'm Scout Lindahl, of Troop #16 of the Panderers, sir. Perhaps I can aid you."

"Perhaps." Gypsy nodded at the gathering of nervous old men. "Better help them first."

"Oh, we've got a whole patrol of Panderers coming for them," Scout Lindahl explained. "I'm a rover, my duty's to take care of loners and strays."

"Who are those old gentlemen?"

"Very wealthy businessmen from all over Europe. This is their semiannual visit to the Riviera." Scout Lindahl smiled. "We're the Fornication Capital of the Known World, you know."

Gypsy nodded.

The Scout continued, "When you grow old, and the juices flow slower, you can get by on a visit every few months. What's your interest, sir?"

Gypsy had been studying the distant bordellos, which

were built in the architectural style of many countries and centuries. "I'm anxious to pay a visit to Madame Potpourri's Establishment."

Scout Lindahl frowned. "I had you down for more adventurous fare," he said, head shaking, scarlet feather fluttering. "What I mean is, the Madame Potpourri outlets are very, very conventional. Not a girl under eighteen in any of them . . ."

"That's okay, the girl I'm looking for doesn't appear to be that young," said Gypsy. "You say there's more than one Madame Potpourri's?"

"Lord, there's seven of them," answered the boy. "It's a franchise operation. Frankly you'll have a much better time of it by trying the Chamber of Commerce Love Casino on Rue—"

"This is the girl I want." Gypsy reached into his tunic for the pamphlet. His right arm, though it didn't look quite as it had, was functioning fairly well since his visit to Balzac yesterday.

"How very sentimental. Almost like those old gents over there." Taking off his cap, Scout Lindahl craned to scrutinize the unfolding Madame Potpourri handout. "Let me give you a friendly word of advice, sir. Don't let on you're eager for a special wench. They'll up the price on you. Bit on the skinny side, isn't she?"

Pointing to the slim, dark-haired girl, Gypsy asked, "Which of Madame Potpourri's places will I find this girl in?"

The Scout edged closer. "That's simple enough, sir. Notice the little number beneath the photo of Amorous Annabelle? 23X-6. A simple code indicating she's in the #6 Establishment. Very gloomy place, built in what is called, I do believe, the Victorian style. You'll find it on the Rue Lazarillo." He gave Gypsy directions.

"Seems like most of your country is given over to

prostitution, with the government and the Chamber of Commerce in on it, too."

"Absolutely, sir. We're the Fornication Capital of the Known World, as I may have mentioned," said the boy. "We can boast of having one of the highest gross nat—"

"Step lively, gents. Step lively." A bunch of Panderers were trotting down the beach toward the old men. "Form a line by twos and follow us."

"It's heartening," said Scout Lindahl, "to see old people still capable of having a bit of fun."

"What about the police," Gypsy asked, "are they part of the system?"

"You can't have a really efficient paid fornication operation without the police in your camp. Yes, sir, all our cribs are very thoroughly policed."

"How thoroughly?"

The boy's eyes narrowed. "There is a highly efficient and well-armed street patrol system. Each and every bordello, of which you'll find two hundred and sixty-one in the immediate vicinity, also has its own police guards. Six to a house. In case of any trouble a large batch of volunteer policemen is also swiftly available. You aren't planning to make any trouble, are you, sir?"

"None, not a bit," Gypsy assured him. "I'm simply a curious sort of individual. You can never learn too much about how things function. Don't you agree?"

Scout Lindahl, backed off three steps. "You're a big, burly fellow," he said. "Even if you claim not to be interested in the byways of sexual experience, sir, I do hope most sincerely you aren't contemplating doing violence to this Amorous Annabelle."

"I'm not."

"Perhaps," suggested the Scout, "I'd better travel along with you, sir. To insure your not getting lost."

"What," asked Gypsy, "is that thing you're reaching

for in your pocket?"

Swallowing, the boy said, "This?" His hand, quivering slightly, emerged clutching a communication box. "This?"

"That," said Gypsy. "Are you planning to alert someone about me? Someone, say, at Madame Potpourri's Establishment #6?"

"The thought had crossed my mind," admitted Scout Lindahl. "You see, sir, when one is inducted into the Panderers one takes an oath, a rather solemn oath, to uphold the honor and integrity of the community. In a community such as ours that means when I suspect someone of planning to bust up one of our whorehouses I—"

"Yeah, okay, I understand." Gypsy narrowed his eyes, focusing his gaze on the black and silver talkbox.

Pop!

The Scout's fingers smacked his empty palm. The talkbox had vanished. "How on earth did—"

"Don't contact anyone about me," Gypsy said. "Not for the next hour anyway. Otherwise you might go where that box went." He gestured at the darkening sea.

"I'll maintain a discreet silence, sir." Hand shaking, he gave a salute.

Gypsy walked away from him.

A platoon of giddy young women in white and scarlet uniforms, went marching down the wide street. The banners they proudly carried identified them as Bimbos, the female counterparts of the Panderers.

The night street was bright, illuminated by lampposts topped with yellow, orange, and crimson globes of light. The signs on the bordellos also glowed brightly.

"Quite explicit, that one." A Japanese businessman in

a four-piece yellow funsuit was taking pictures of one of the animated light-signs.

"Very nasty," said his companion, a Japanese businessman in a matching four-piece yellow jumper.

Gypsy passed them, following in the wake of the marching Bimbos. Madame Potpourri's Establishment #6 lay ahead on the opposite corner. A three-story building, constructed of real wood, rich with turrets and cupolas and gingerbread trim.

He stopped on the curb, studying the façade of the place. There was no evidence of extra police, though he had seen some of the white-clad lawmen patrolling the streets as he made his way here. Gypsy didn't sense any trouble awaiting him inside Madame Potpourri's. So quite probably Scout Lindahl had been sufficiently frightened and hadn't warned anyone about the possible trouble Gypsy might cause.

An oaken front door opened in anticipation of Gypsy although he was still three steps away from it. "Full up at the moment, sir." A thin woman with a grey face and wearing a purple bathrobe peered out at him.

"Is there a waiting list?"

"There surely is," the woman admitted through the narrow opening. "You want my advice, I wouldn't bother to sign. There's forty-seven of those Japanese tourist gentlemen ahead of you. By the time they get finished, what with cavorting and snapping photos, you'll be lucky to get a turn much before dawn."

He stepped onto the thermal doormat. "I've traveled a long way," he confided, producing the advertising pamphlet. "Driven by one of your handouts, ma'am."

"Isn't that sweet." She watched his hands as the pamphlet was unfolded. "You'd be surprised at how little sweetness and sentimentality I see on any given business day."

"With me," continued Gypsy, "it was what you might call love at first sight. When I cast my eyes on this picture of Amorous Annabelle I was—"

"Oh, her." The grey woman's face grew grim and sour. "Your money would be better spent on another."

Gypsy moved forward and into the bordello hallway, forcing the woman to back up. "Is there something wrong with her?"

The hall was thick with tables, hatracks, and umbrella stands. The woman rubbed at the marble tabletop of the nearest clawfoot. "She's not too experienced," she said.

"Excellent. An unspoiled maiden from—"

"She's not *that* inexperienced," the woman said. "What it is, she's not taking to the routine of Madame Potpourri's too well."

"I was led to believe," said Gypsy, rattling the brochure while pushing further into the establishment, "that she was, to quote your description, 'passionate and fiery, eager for—' "

"Oh, you know how copywriters are. Make up any old thing, slap it into print. What do they care what they promise?"

"The girl is here, isn't she?"

"That she is. But I'd advise you to—"

Thump! Thump!

Tingle!

Wang!

Music had commenced in the parlor on her right. "Who turned on that thing? Turn it off."

Tingle!

Wang! Wam!

The raucous piano music continued.

"All these contraptions." The grey woman pushed aside the beaded curtains and charged into the parlor. "If it isn't the porn-stereoscope going on the blink, it's this

darn robot pianoman."

Gypsy followed her into the pink and gold room.

A sturdy, copper-plated robot, with two left arms and one right, was pounding out a ragtime tune on the ornately carved upright piano. He wore a derby tilted on his ball-shaped head.

A small, elderly man in a brand-new two-piece funsuit was seated on a striped loveseat across the room. "I didn't *touch* him," he said. "I was merely sitting alone here awaiting the advent of Tempestuous Terri and he—"

"Stop! Quit! Lay off!" The woman thumped the robot's metal back with both fists.

Gypsy backed out of the parlor as the music continued. Out in the hall again he stood still for several seconds, eyes nearly shut. "She's on the second floor," he decided.

At the top of the stairs, his hairy fist clutching the white newel post, stood a man in half a police uniform. "Where's your mark?" he asked.

"Where's your pants?"

"That is neither here nor there, chum." The large cop showed the star stamped on his palm to Gypsy. "You got to pay your entry fee, see, and then you get stamped like this. Otherwise I toss you."

Gypsy opened his right hand. "I've got the stamped mark, sure enough."

"I don't see any . . . oof!"

Gypsy kept his hand moving upward until it smacked the guard hard across the nose. The policeman went tottering back. Gypsy leaped, catching him by his coat. He reached back and squeezed the burly man's neck. The man wilted.

Spreading the unconscious guard out on the flowered carpeting of the landing, Gypsy continued on. He had more than a strong hunch that Annabelle was in a room

around the next bend in the corridor.

"Find the dad-ratted thing!"

"Where'd you have it last, Count Primo?"

"How do I know? When I was thrashing that newsboy at the corner of Proust and Racine. No, wait . . . I distinctly recall having it in hand when I entered this dodgasted place this evening. Yes, because I took a swipe at the old lady with it."

Coming around the bend, Gypsy encountered a large, ruddy man in a five-piece black and crimson eveningsuit. He carried a black satchel, had a mace tucked up under one arm, a cat-o'-nine-tails dangling from a hip pocket. Standing near him was a valet-robot who'd been painted a cocoa-brown color.

"Haven't seen my horsewhip lying about, young fella?"

"No, sorry."

"Going to need it," said Count Primo. "Busy night ahead of me." He raised the satchel until its handle was level with his connecting eyebrows. "Brought the full kit to use on this dad-blasted female. What's her dod-busted name again?"

"You have the work order, Count," the cocoa-brown robot informed him.

"Clearly remember handing it to you," said the count reflectively. "Yes, handed it to you while we were en route. 'Hold this dad-blasted whorehouse brochure, Elmo, until I'm finished thrashing this disrespectful flower vendor.' Clearly remember saying that."

"Indeed you did," said Elmo. "However, sir, I returned it to you when I stooped to pick the old lady out of the gutter and prop her up against the flower cart."

"A sentimental, and unnecessary, gesture."

Gypsy asked, "You've been *asked* to thrash someone here at Madame Potpourri's?"

"*Hired* is more the dad-bangled size of it, young fella," said Count Primo. "Once in a while they get a girl who's a bit reluctant. That's when Count Primo is called in. Spend a few hours with the piece of goods, a good bit of persuading. They usually come around to the proper way of thinking after an evening with me, sir. Of course, they're never *sincere* about it."

"Would your job tonight, by any chance, involve a girl named Annabelle?"

"It well might," replied the count. "Elmo, where is that dod-boggled brochure with the young lady's picture in it?"

"If you but search your pockets, Count, you'll—"

"Dad-rat it, Elmo, I've sixteen pockets in this suit. I'm not going to stand in a whorehouse hallway and search through sixteen—"

"I believe that's the prospectus I see peeping out of your vest pocket."

"Which?"

"There, with the bamboo slivers."

"So it . . . aii! Got to be more careful with these bamboo slivers, keep sticking them under my own dod-blasted nails." He flicked his wrist and the brochure flapped open. "See if you can read off the name of the young person they've circled for my attentions this evening, Elmo. I seem to have misplaced my monocle when we were giving that shoestring vendor a piece of our mind."

"I believe he smashed the lens with his crutch ferrule during the struggle, Count." The robot took the pamphlet. "Here is the girl in question . . . Amorous Annabelle. 'Very uncooperative' is scribbled in the margin along with the notation that she is ensconced in the Algernon Swinburne Suite."

"Which we are about to enter, soon as we locate my horsewhip," the count told Gypsy.

"I myself," said Gypsy, "prefer a cat-o'-nine-tails."
He snatched the whip out of the count's rear pocket.

"Here now, sir!" cautioned the robot.

Gypsy caught the count by the shoulders, spun him
around and gave him several light strokes of the whip
across the backside. The count lost his balance, fell,
rolled, much like an orange, down the corridor and
around the bend.

"WHAT'S GOING ON . . . *Oof!*"

From the sound of it, the police guard had come to and
had been in the process of running after Gypsy when the
rolling count collided into him.

"I ought to warn you," said the robot, "I have a stungun built into my left arm." The arm started to swing up.

"Quit!" said Gypsy.

The mechanism went dead.

Nodding in satisfaction that at least some of his
abilities were working well, Gypsy took hold of the handle of Annabelle's door.

Spiders roamed the vast terrace, the stone wall of which they'd long since festooned with webs. It was a moonless night, and the scurrying creatures made spots of deeper black on the dark stones.

"I'll be okay," Annabelle was saying. "You forget how quickly I bounce back, Gypsy." She was resting in a rusted wrought-iron chair which Gypsy had furnished with pillows borrowed from inside the deserted villa.

"You'll be well enough to move on tomorrow?" He was sitting, cross-legged, on the flagstones near her.

"Oh, am I part of the Gypsy traveling circus again?"

Keeping his eyes on the black ocean far below, he said, "When you're on your own you tend to get into—"

"*I* tend to? Listen, luv, before I encountered you a few weeks ago back in merrie olde England, I was just a simple, fun-loving, everyday—"

"Crook," he supplied.

"Admittedly I was running with bad company. But the Queen Bess group was more than a gang of thieves. She had—"

"Higher goals, I know. Including the wiping out of every male in Great Britain."

"That was her idea, not mine." She was dressed in a simple tunic and shorts outfit, her smooth legs bare. "I was in that gang because it looked like a way to get regular meals and—"

"How did Madame Potpourri get hold of you?"

"That's your bloody fault, too."

"Oh, so?" He glanced across at her, grinning.

"You left me sitting there on Gibraltar while you went off on your blessed quest. . . . Did you learn anything new, by the way?"

Nodding, Gypsy said, "Finish your story, I'll tell you later."

"I waited and I waited on Gibraltar after you left. Even after Walpole took off—I assume to join you—I

stuck there a few more days. But finally I—"

"Wait now, Walpole never joined me. Did he tell you I sent for him?"

"Nope, he simply up and disappeared. I figured the two of you had ditched me."

"There was no plan to abandon you, Annabelle. No plan for Walpole to join me."

"I suppose right now you were hurrying back to Gibraltar when you got sidetracked into a side trip to the Riviera?"

Gypsy said, "As a matter of fact I was en route to Africa."

"And I was supposed to wait on Gibraltar with all those agriculture buffs until that jaunt was completed? Or were you planning to—"

"Annabelle, I still think you ought to stay on the sidelines for awhile." He frowned, shook his head. "Things are going to get rougher."

"*Rougher?* When I'm separated from you I almost get burned for a witch in Spain," the girl said, "and then I get recruited for a brothel by a roving gang of burly, extremely persuasive, pimps. What worse can befall me if I tag along with you?" She reached over, caught his right hand. "Besides which . . . Gypsy, did you get hurt rescuing me?"

"No, this happened earlier. The patch-up job is a little rough."

"Sounds like you've had some colorful experiences, too."

"I've found out more about myself," he answered after a few silent seconds. "But not enough. The hand isn't real."

Annabelle didn't let go. "Oh?"

"Whole forearm isn't real. I learned that in a place called Villedeux, a well-ordered little country ruled, until recently, by robots."

"You had something to do with their fall from power."

"I helped the humans get control, yes. Although I'm wondering—been wondering since. . . . How was I able to do all that I did?"

"What do you mean?"

"Something happened to me, remember? Put me into some sort of coma for over a half century. Who knows *what* was done to me?"

The girl shook her head violently. "I don't believe it's that serious. You have a mechanical arm, okay. So do a good many other people."

"But what *did* happen to me, Annabelle? Who am I? What *happened* to me?"

"There must be a way to find out for good and all," she said. "I mean, without going on this quest of yours, without playing this game. Is that vicious vulture still tailing you?"

"Haven't seen him since Villedeux," Gypsy answered. "Consider that vulture. It has some of the same powers I do . . . it can teleport, has telekinetic ability. The damn thing can even talk."

Her grip on his hand tightened. "That may just mean it had something important to do with who you were—*are*."

"Definitely—I think this Dr. Hawksworth, the scientist who figures in my past back in the twentieth century, I think *she* built the vulture." He looked quietly up at Annabelle. "There's a man, Wondersmith, an inventor. He has, so I'm told, one of the few X-ray machines in this part of what's left of the world."

"An *X-ray*? Then he can look inside you," said Annabelle. "Yes, that's a good idea. You'll be able to settle part of this business. You'll see if there are any devices inside you—see if—"

"No matter what Wondersmith's X-ray proves, I have to keep on with the quest."

"No, you don't, Gypsy, there's no—"

"Okay, listen," he said, standing up and extricating his hand from hers. "No matter what the machine shows me, that still doesn't tell me who I actually am. Why did I wake up in Paris fifty years after the last date I remember? Who am I, really?"

"You're *Gypsy*! Isn't that enough for you to know?"

"You know it's not." He paced, moving nearer the low wall of the terrace. He'd passed this abandoned villa on his way to the Riviera, remembered it when he needed a place to halt and look after the girl. "I am obviously something other than a normal human being. What? Why? To what purpose?"

"Very metaphysical," remarked Annabelle.

He spun to face her, his broad back to the dark ocean below. "Come on, Annabelle, you'd do the same thing. You wouldn't sit back and not care about . . . about your identity."

"Possibly." The girl shrugged her slim shoulders. "Where does this Wondersmith guy hang out?"

"He's on the island of Corsica."

Annabelle left her chair, walking a bit unsteadily, and went to the terrace wall. "What about Walpole? Where do you think he's gone to?"

"I haven't any . . ." The sentence died. Gypsy's lips pressed together, his forehead creased.

The girl went to him. "What is it? What's wrong?"

"Something . . . vague." He put an arm around Annabelle to steady her. "Something . . . about Walpole. There's some kind of trouble—your mention of him—Walpole is in danger."

"Where?"

Shaking his head, Gypsy answered, "I don't know,

Annabelle, but Corsica seems like our best chance at making some discoveries right now—maybe there'll be some word on Walpole, too."

"Then off to Corsica," said the girl, "with the dawn."

The morning sun was bright, the sky and the sea both clear and glistening blue. Arm in arm, Gypsy and Annabelle were walking along a bright yellow boardwalk which led to a boat marina. The white beach on their right was empty, no one was swimming in the ocean.

"It's just," Gypsy was explaining, "that I don't feel completely comfortable with my powers anymore. So we'd better travel to Corsica in a more conventional way."

"Well, ocean travel is supposed to be romantic," said the girl. "Do you think we'll be able to hire some kind of boat around here?"

"The folks at the last fishing village indicated as much."

"Yeah, but they struck me as a bit spooky," Annabelle said. "Especially when they discussed this town. Macabreville . . . not the most cheerful name in the world."

Up on their immediate left loomed an immense seaside hotel. It rose ten stories, was painted a flat, somber black. The name *Macabreville Ritz* was stitched in large silver letters on the black awning over the main entrance. At the moment they passed the black-tinted glass doors of the hotel, those doors flapped open and a large scruffy man in a rumpled black suit was tossed out by two bellhops in grey uniforms.

Before the big scruffy man pushed himself up from the planks of the boardwalk a grey-gloved hand taped a freshly lettered sign to one of the glass doors—*Under New Management*.

"There goes my convention," complained the newly ejected man.

Gypsy had paused to help him gather himself together. "Having some trouble with the new management?"

"Worse than that," replied the man, thrusting out his

large lower lip. "But then what can one expect in a world like this. A world, if I may elaborate, which has been visited by a series of devastating wars, a few dozen revolutions, sundry plagues and famines, and now teeters on the brink of extinction. As do we all, we poor mortals." He made a slight, wobbly bow. "I happen to be, in case you didn't immediately recognize me, none other than Professor Xavier Xanadu. Yes, the man who wrote *Doom*, as well as *More Doom, Doom Revisited, The Best of Doom*, and many more. Not that writing books makes any sense—the worms'll devour them faster than my own poor carcass."

"You don't *look* like you're being devoured," remarked Annabelle.

"I speak of what *will* happen to me, young lady, once I am in my tomb. Then—and it won't be long—the grave worms will have their way," explained Professor Xanadu. "What is more immediately fearful to contemplate is the fact I've been given the old heave-ho by the new owners of the Macabreville Ritz. This certainly means we'll have to hold the Fifth Annual Deathcon elsewhere."

Gypsy and Annabelle had resumed walking. The professor fell in with them.

"You're planning some sort of convention?" the girl asked.

"Haven't you heard of Xanadu's Deathcons? Why, in the poor fragments of once proud and powerful Europe my yearly festivities are famed and fabled," the large professor informed her. "Now the new powers that be have decided we're too morbid for Macabreville. How can anything in this life be too morbid? What, after all, are we but living reminders of our eventual sad ends? I should have suspected after the last election, when all those jovial new selectmen were voted in, that the days of

the Deathcon in Macabreville were numbered."

"A town with a name like Macabreville," said Annabelle, "you'd expect the people to be just your type."

"The new boys are even thinking about changing the town's name," sighed Xanadu. "Well, my primary concern at the moment is to get to the yacht and—"

"You have a yacht?" asked Gypsy.

"How else can I transport six white horses, a funeral coach, nineteen professional mourners, a 242-pound corpse, and a staff of sixteen around the Mediterranean?"

"A corpse?" said the girl. "Has someone near and dear to you passed on?"

"No, never met the fellow, but his family kindly donated him to us," replied the professor. "A full and dramatic funeral is always the culminating event in any of my three-day Deathcons. One of the things which brings death fans from all over this region of our dying and decayed world is the chance to see a real slam-bang funeral. When civilization started to go really blooey, a good many countries dropped their time-honored burial practices. Drop 'em in a hole and cover 'em up, that was good enough. What else can you expect in such an imperfect world."

Gypsy inquired, "Are you going to be scouting for a new convention site?"

"Immediately, yes. Then I'll have to rush new ads into all the deathzines, alert all my guests and all the memento mori and morbid book dealers of the new location," said Xanadu. "The scheduled date is only three weeks off. We're also expecting seven of the best surviving tombstone cutters. That's going to need room, what with a display of monuments as part of the show. Some of those babies, the ones with angels and all, are immense. There's a chance we'll have old Cochran himself as Guest

of Honor, the man who bought up Forest Lawn in America to sell as souvenirs. What a coup for him, what a collection!"

"Would you," Gypsy said, "be sailing in the direction of Corsica?"

"Should pass right by it," said the Deathcon promoter. "One of my first stops will be on the coast near there, place where they're still very partial to morbidity. I sometimes stage some of my smaller one-day cons there. May I offer you a lift?"

"We'd appreciate it," said Gypsy, "since we're anxious to get to the island."

"Business reasons? Romance?"

"We want to visit our grandmother's grave," said Annabelle. "That's always fun."

"Yes, *isn't* it?" agreed Professor Xanadu. "I'm very fortunate in having, on my late mother's side, a grandfather who married six very-short-lived ladies at various stages of his career. This provides me with, on the maternal side alone, an even half-dozen grandmother graves to visit."

"When will you be leaving, Professor?"

"The sooner the better. There's my ship moored over there, the large black one."

"Very grim," murmured Annabelle.

"Why, thank you," said Xanadu. "It serves to remind us of how very easily we might all perish at sea. Sink without a trace! Have the vile creatures of the deep pick at our bones!"

"At least that way," added Annabelle with a half-cocked smile, "you'd avoid those worms."

"Death has so many guises," said Xavier Xanadu, "if you avoid him in one, you run smack into him in another. But enough of this, come aboard. With any luck, you'll be just in time for the wake."

The man in the black sailor suit had a firm grip on the chubby girl's right ear. "You'll answer to the professor, young missy."

"Snarf yourself, you walleyed brucie."

The sailor halted on the threshold of Xanadu's cabin. "What's that you said, missy? What'd you call me?"

The teenaged girl, eyes made up with black half-circles beneath them, wore a simple two-piece black neonylon shift, black kneeboots, and a black headband. "I referred to you as a walleyed brucie, you big limp."

"Wait a sec. Am I correct in assuming such words as brucie and limp imply something about my sexual outlook? For if so, I hasten to—"

"Vivian," the professor called to the sailor, "what are you up to?"

"I caught this young missy in the hold, a stowaway she is."

"Vivian?" The chubby girl snorted. "*There's* a brucie name if I—"

"She was all hunkered down among the cases of votive candles, sir."

"Let her go and shoo her in here, Viv." Turning to the seated Gypsy and Annabelle, Xanadu said, "Excuse me while I look into this stowaway matter."

"I'm no stowaway," insisted the girl while overcoming the effects of the black-clad sailor's shove into the room. "I'm simply a deathie."

The professor rubbed at his ill-shaved jaw. "So are all mortals, alas, though few realize it," he said. "A deathie, eh, a devoted Deathcon fan? Even so, young lady, I can't allow you to travel aboard my ship."

"But I'm one of the top Deathcon buffs in this part of the remaining world. I'm Bettsy Weber, editor of *Deathzine*."

"Are you indeed? You wrote a very perceptive review

of our last cremation marathon, Miss Weber," said Professor Xanadu. "Nevertheless, it is my steadfast policy not to allow fans to frequent the yacht. There's too much potential for trouble, even scandal."

"If I were you, Prof, I'd worry about the scandal that's going to hit when *Deathzine* prints my account of all the brucies you've got aboard."

"Sir, if I might say a word in my defense," put in Vivian, who lingered in the doorway.

Xanadu reached out to pat the skull atop his desk. "Never mind, Viv. We all have to learn to live with the slurs of the press."

Annabelle moved out of her chair very carefully, so as not to rattle the skeleton hanging from a gold chain immediately beside her. "Where did you come on board, Bettsy?"

"At Macabreville. I was sleeping peacefully down in the hold when a whole lot of howling woke me up."

"That was only the wailing and keening," said the sailor. "For the wake."

"I'm not a big fan of that end of mourning," said the chubby girl.

"Do you have parents?" asked Annabelle.

"Worse luck, yes. Half of the subscribers to *Deathzine* have at least one deceased parent, a few are full-time complete orphans. But me, my mom and pop are both hale and hearty. In fact, my father—"

"Scoundrel ahoy!"

Professor Xanadu bounded from his chair. "What in the—"

"Oh, it's only my father," said Bettsy, her black-rimmed eyes turning upward. "Darned if he hasn't got the killship out again."

"*Killship*?" The professor cleared his throat. "Your parental parent is a deathie, too? Calls his craft a—"

"No, he named it that because he uses it so much to kill wild animals from," explained the girl. "And occasionally people, when they make him very mad."

Vivian was watching the late afternoon sky above. "Some sort of hovering aircraft, sir. Hovering about two hundred feet above your cabin."

"Ahoy down there, you blithering woop!"

The professor frowned at the chubby girl. *"Woop*? Is that more of this adolescent slang?"

"Nope." Bettsy shook her head. "Dad likes to use a lot of slang expressions from his own wild and untamed youth, when he was a strangler in the Bombay Enclave. Being called a woop . . . I don't think that's so good."

"Return my daughter unharmed and unmolested!"

"People he refers to as woops," pursued the professor, "are they the ones he tends to kill?"

"If memory serves me rightly, yes."

"He's coming down closer," warned Vivian.

"Return my daughter or your yacht will be blown to dust!"

"Ah, the eventual fate of us all," sighed Xanadu.

Gypsy left his chair, circled the coffin net to the professor's ebony desk, and stepped out onto the glistening black deck. The killship was the size of a rowboat, but sleek and cylindrical, painted a bright orange. There was a plyoglass viewing hole in its underside and an angry, flushed face was pressed against it. Gypsy waved at the girl's father. "You want the girl back, is *that* it?"

"Don't go making obscene gestures at me, laddy boy!"

"You can have her back right now," Gypsy shouted through cupped hands.

"Is this some sort of trap?" The hovering Weber's voice roared out of the bellyspeakers of his killship. *"How do I know you won't pull some cute trick once I set down?"*

"No need to land." Gypsy beckoned to the girl.

"I'm determined to stick things out," she told him. "I've every right to be on this darned morbid yacht as—"

"And I want to get to Corsica. If the professor's yacht is destroyed, it'll delay me." Gypsy, eyes narrowing, stared at the girl. His fingers clenched.

She was gone.

"You're all a bunch of brucies," Bettsy accused. Her voice was coming out of the killship now.

Her father's face left the viewhole. The ship made a fluting sound before arcing away through the afternoon.

"How," asked Xanadu, venturing onto the deck, "did you accomplish that?"

Gypsy shrugged, saying, "It's just something I can do."

Professor Xanadu ran his tongue over his substantial lower lip. "This has been a very satisfying occurrence," he said. "Scrapes with death always are."

"At least he doesn't have to worry about the neighbors bothering him," said Annabelle.

"From what they told us down in the village, most people admire Wondersmith but don't want to get too close."

Gypsy and the girl were climbing a narrow dirt road. It was dusk, the rocky hills all around them were turning black, as were the few leafless trees. There were no houses visible, no huts or shacks.

"Professor Xanadu ought to hold a convention here—it's bleak enough." Annabelle got a firmer grip on his arm.

Gypsy smiled. "That was one of the more interesting boat trips in my experience," he said. "At least those that I can remember."

"Don't go getting morbid like the prof."

"Having a past which only stretches back a few weeks. . . . That must be Wondersmith's chateau. On the bluffs up there."

The place was large, judging from the lighted windows which showed. Two stories high, at least.

"It's all self-contained," said the girl. "He has his own generators and everything?"

"Correct. So if Wondersmith's willing, I should find . . . *Good* . . ." Gypsy's voice trailed off in mid-sentence. The road beneath their feet was suddenly vibrating with the force of a rocket. He and Annabelle instinctively grabbed for the security of each other's body, but before they could get a sure footing, there was an enormous flash up ahead.

The chateau, which was still a half-mile up the road from them, suddenly began to come apart. An enormous red flash swelled out of the middle of the building, tearing it into great black fragments. A gigantic whomping roar came barreling down the hillside.

"You better wait here," Gypsy told the girl. "No telling—"

"Like heck. I'm coming along."

He began to run, she kept up with him. "A damn powerful explosion," he said. "I don't think there's going to be much left of the chateau."

"Or of Wondersmith."

"Let's hope he wasn't inside."

The pieces of the chateau had returned to earth, and now flames were spewing up into the new blackness of the night. Gypsy and the girl were coming close enough to hear the crackle of the flames.

Then, from behind the ruins of the building, an airship rose up like nothing Gypsy had ever seen. It was sleek, silvery, long-nosed and snub-winged. It moved upward into the night with absolutely no noise and went arcing away from the remains of the Wondersmith lab in seconds.

"Down!" Gypsy shouted when he first spotted the craft. With an arm around Annabelle, he flattened out on the road.

The airship paid them no mind, but kept on climbing away from them and away from the destroyed chateau and from the Corsica coastline.

After a moment Gypsy scrambled to his feet and then assisted the girl to hers.

"Would that have been Wondersmith making a hasty departure?" she asked.

"Dunno." He caught her hand and they went racing for the burning ruins.

They found Wondersmith in the courtyard, his lower half crushed beneath rock and timbers. He was a massive old man, his long white hair tangled and smeared now. And he was alive. When Gypsy knelt beside him he said, "You took . . . everything . . . what . . ."

"No—I came to help you," Gypsy said, as he very carefully removed the debris pinning down the old man.

"Waste of time," Wondersmith said in a dry, distant voice. "They got what they wanted . . . everything . . . of . . . been watching . . . watching . . . waiting . . . didn't even know it . . . stupid . . ."

"Who? Who were they?"

"Don't you know?" His eyelids lowered. "It was . . . the Scavengers." Then he died.

Gypsy stood up and moved away. "Too late," he said. "Too damn late—because I was afraid to use my abilities. Afraid to try teleporting here. He could have beat them."

"And maybe they'd have blown you and me up along with that poor old man."

"The Scavengers . . ." Gypsy muttered. "The Scavengers—never heard of them. You?"

"Nope." She shook her head. "But they don't sound like a friendly bunch, judging from what they've done here."

"What *have* they done here, though?" Hands on hips, he surveyed the ruins. "Did they destroy all of Wondersmith's inventions?"

"No—he told you they'd *taken* everything, remember?"

"Yeah, that's right. What kind of organization is it? . . . The Scavengers . . ."

"They're not my kind of scavengers," said a rasping, mocking voice.

Whirling, Gypsy faced the vulture. It was hunched on a branch of a gnarled tree a few feet away from them. Eyes gleaming in the flicker of the fire, beak slightly open. "What did *you* have to do with this?" Gypsy demanded.

"Easy does it, Gyp, me lad," advised the bird. "I don't murder people, I only clean up afterward. This was not

my doing."

"Then why are you here?" Gypsy's hands turned to fists as he stalked closer to the tree.

"Looking after business, Gypo," replied the bird. "I'm your mentor, so to speak, practically the only family you have left in this world."

"You killed Wondersmith," accused Gypsy, jabbing a finger at him. "Killed him so I couldn't—"

"That's not a bad patch job they did on your arm, old buddy."

"Wondersmith had an X-ray machine, and so you didn't want me to—"

"Will you *quit*, for crying out loud, being such a ninny!" The vulture turned its eyes toward the girl. "Maybe you can reason with him, Sis. Explain to old Gyp I'm on his side."

"*First* I'd like to believe that myself," she said.

"When," Gypsy asked the vulture, "did you arrive here?"

"Too late to stop anything," the bird replied. "Much too late to have caused this unpleasantness."

"So *you* say."

"He really doesn't appreciate me," the hunched bird remarked to Annabelle.

Gypsy said, "I came here to Corsica to consult Wondersmith, to find out—"

"Yes, yes, I know. Doesn't seem sporting to me, Gyp, smacking as it does of cutting corners."

"I'm getting tired of your damned game, of—"

"It's not *my* game, dear boy. I'm not even, despite what you may think in mean-minded moments, a referee."

"I'm damned impatient, I want answers." Gypsy lifted up his right arm, smacked it with his left hand, hard, several times. "This is a *fake*! *Why*?"

The vulture extended its wings, regripped its perch,

folded the huge black wings. "I have more important stuff to talk about, Gyp."

"The hell with you. I may as well go on to Africa, to follow up the clue I dug up at Villedeux. With Wondersmith dead, all his equipment destroyed, there's no—"

"You're missing the point, don't be a dunce," said the bird. "Most of the late Wondersmith's mechanisms —and *all* of his most clever inventions—were taken by the Scavengers before they blew up the joint."

"Okay, tell me about them," said Gypsy. "Who are the Scavengers, and what are they up to?"

"You might say they're, as the name implies, *collectors*," began the vulture. "Actually, they're more than that. The Scavengers are a secret and clandestine outfit, with several bases hidden around the world. For the past several years, especially during the time you were napping away, Gyp, they've been recruiting scientists, technicians, mercenaries, and plain old simple opportunists. The Scavengers roam the world, such as it is, raiding and looting. Whenever they hear of a new weapon, a cache of pre-Collapse hardware, or some plunder, they move. Usually they operate in the style you came in on the tail end of today."

"I've never heard of them," said Gypsy.

"There are a multitude of things you haven't heard of, my boy."

"Do they have a purpose," asked Annabelle, "beyond simple looting?"

"Indeed they do, missy," answered the bird, with a rattling chuckle. "Theirs is an old, old ambition. Very trite, yet they are going to give it a whirl anyhow. When they have sufficient funds, sufficient artillery . . . they'll make their big move. They intend to take over all the existing countries, rule them as one empire."

"Nobody's ever brought *that* off," said Annabelle.

"Ah, but lots of fun can be had in trying," the vulture pointed out. "At any rate, such is what the Scavengers are about."

Gypsy nodded slowly. "Okay, they're a nasty bunch, they upset my plans. Now, though, they're gone and I can get on with the quest. I don't see how the Scavengers have much to do with me."

"There you're wrong again, Gyp." The great bird cackled with amusement. "They know all about you, these Scavengers do. They haven't made an overt move against you so far because they're a mite afraid of you. Not sure of all your powers, all your little tricks. But trust me, they fully intend to add you to their collection."

"What does *that* mean?"

"They collect *people*, too. Wondersmith was killed, rather than taken, because he put up a fight defending his lab. When it came to a choice between the old inventor and his new inventions, they picked the hardware."

"Even if the Scavengers know about me," said Gypsy, "until now I've avoided them, and I can probably keep doing so for as long as I want."

"That's a possibility," the vulture conceded, "yet there's one other fact you ought to know. They've already collected your chum Walpole."

"What the hell are you talking about?"

"The Scavengers have teleported that whimsical and erratic youth to one of their hidden bases, and at this very moment are questioning him," said the vulture. "They wish to know more about you, and Walpole knows some interesting things."

"Which base is he being held—"

"Try the Cape Verde Islands, unless you're too anxious to return to the game, Gyp. In which case, Africa is—"

"*Which* island?"

The vulture's wings commenced flapping.

Gypsy sprinted, jumped, and tried to grab at its twisted feet.

It eluded him, flew straight up and away into the night.

"Is that true," said Annabelle, "what it told you about Walpole?"

"That creature," said Gypsy slowly, "never lies to me."

SEVEN

They had him in a snug, cozy parlor. A small room with thick flowered carpets over the hardwood floor, much rich and highly polished nineteenth-century furniture. A pleasant fire burning in the brick fireplace.

Walpole was sprawled on the oval rug nearest the crackling logs, his legs bent, his fingers digging into the endlessly repeated rose pattern. "I've told you," he said, "every perishing thing I know about everything." His voice was raw, a shade squeaky. His face and hands were streaked with dry blood.

"Tell us again." A plump, blonde young man sat in a bentwood rocker, rocking gently. He had a cherubic, beatific face. Across his plump knees rested a newly invented type of stunrod. "We enjoy hearing it, over and over, Mr. Walpole."

"You ruddy sadist. Your flapping machines have already ground all the info out of me. So there's—"

"Tell us *again*." The other man in the parlor kicked the fallen Walpole in the ribs. He was tall, broad, his skin a very pale white, his beard a glistening blue-black. "*Again!*"

The boot dug once again into one of the sore spots in Walpole's side. "Keep your blasted feet to yourself, mate."

"Come on, tell us again," urged the plump young man. "Begin with how you met Gypsy."

"Why don't you just play your bloody tapes. I ain't . . . Ah!"

The tall man kicked him another time. "How did you meet Gypsy?"

"Someday I'll stuff that perishing boot straight up your arse," Walpole promised.

"Could you—do you—think you could turn your head a bit, Mr. Walpole? We're losing some of your words into the carpet."

Spitting out lint and a little blood, Walpole said, "I met Gypsy in London."

"How did that come about?"

"We bumped into each other, you might say. I was dodging the bobbies at the time."

"And what was Gypsy doing?"

"Looking for himself."

"Don't be wise," warned the booted man.

"That's the ruddy trouble with you Scavenger blokes." Walpole, with considerable effort, managed to push himself up until he was resting on one elbow. "No feel for the English language, no ear for style and our bloody nuance. I was telling you that Gypsy was interested in finding out more concerning his background."

"*Did* he, Mr. Walpole?"

"Come off it, mate. You know wanking well he did," Walpole told the blonde young man. "Your ruddy machines, your robots and the rest, have been putting me through the wringer! Your medics have pumped me full of truth drugs. By this time you ought to know more about me and Gypsy than I do."

"Keep talking," the other man advised.

"Okay, old top, okay. If you want me whole perishing autobiography, so be it," said Walpole. "I was born, of humble parents and in humble circumstances, in the year 2007 in a little . . . ouch!"

"*Gypsy*," said the booted man. "We only wish to hear of *him*."

"I met Gypsy while avoiding a Newgatewagon, which is a landvan the bobbies in London 3 tool about in," continued the lanky young man. "We hit it off, so to speak, and became buddies. We kicked around hither and yon, then you buggers got your dabs on me with some kind of mumbo-jumbo process or other. Some bloody kind of teleportation it was."

"Yes, a simple teleportation gun," said the blonde young man. "Quite an effective range, and one of the many, many unusual devices we have at our disposal."

"After I was popped here from the boat you put me on against me will, you chaps took to me with your bloomin' unusual devices. That's the whole story, mates."

"More about *Gypsy*!" Another kick.

"Yes, Mr. Walpole, please *do* fill us in on the specifics of what you did once you'd joined forces with Gypsy."

Walpole attempted, as best he could, to shift to a more comfortable position. He couldn't find one. "We traveled the English countryside, had a bit of a tussle with a group of lady revolutionaries headed up by a rather odd sparrow name of Queen Bess. Gypsy fixed her wagon, and we was able to keep them from killing off a good portion of the male populace of the Isles with a little thing known as the Plague."

"A shame Gypsy destroyed the supplies and the formula," said the plump young man with a sigh. "The Scavengers had their eye on the Plague—but, alas! we were not swift enough."

"Would have been useful," added the other man.

"*Useful*? Bloody *useful* that stuff is."

"It might have come in handy," said the blonde young man. "Now, *please*, Mr. Walpole, continue with your narrative."

"All right. After England, Gypsy and I hopped down to Gibraltar . . . might we still be near Gibraltar, this underground hideaway?"

"We might. Please, do go on."

"Nothing much more to tell, old cork. I decided to continue on by meself, having concluded I was no longer interested in Gypsy's perishing quest."

"Not true," said the booted man.

"Okay, okay, so I wanted to be off for a bit, to do

some thinking," admitted Walpole. "Before I got much of that done, you chaps got hold of me."

The plump young man said, "We understand this friend of yours has a good many special abilities and talents."

"You understand correctly, mate."

"More details." The big man booted him once more in the side.

"Why don't you give me a shot of something. I don't like to peach on my friends right out in the open like this."

"Mr. Walpole, we have already, as you are aware, used truth drugs and mechanisms on you. This little get-together today is to catch any little details which our sometimes fallible machines may have missed." The plump, blonde Scavenger rocked a few times. "You've already betrayed Gypsy, against your will but nonetheless. Don't put yourself through further painful experiences simply to hold back information we probably already have."

After almost a minute Walpole said, "Gypsy has what you call, I guess, psi powers. I mean to say, he can move objects from place to place. Sometimes he can lift a thing up, such as that godawful lamp on yonder godawful table, and put her down somewheres else. But the object, you know, never goes out of your sight. Other times he can simply send the bloody thing off someplace. From that table to London 3—or anywhere."

"His telekinetic capabilities we're aware of. What else can Gypsy do?"

Walpole poked his tongue into his cheek. "I don't know all the powers he's got, nor does the gov. One thing, he can move himself. Or me with him, for that matter. All he needs to do is grab hold of you and you go popping off from one spot to another."

"Need it be," inquired the big man, "a place Gypsy has visited before?"

"I don't think so, mate. When we jumped to Madrid . . . he'd never laid eyes on the blooming place before. Far as he knows . . ." Walpole let the sentence fade.

"He's having some trouble with his memory, isn't he?"

"I didn't actual *say* that."

"But you already have," the plump, blonde young man pointed out. "We merely want to hear the story again."

Walpole took a deep breath, which caused him some pain due to the condition of his ribs and side. Grimacing, he answered, "Gypsy don't quite remember who he is."

"Yes, go on."

"What can I ruddy go on with? He ain't got much of an idea who he is. It's amnesia like."

"He knows his name."

"Gypsy ain't exactly first and last name and middle initial, is it now? And a bloke may know his perishing nickname without he knows exactly who he might be. There's more to a chap's identity than the name they hang on him."

"Very good observation," said the big man. "How much has Gypsy found out so far?"

Walpole rubbed his hand, gingerly, along his side. "He knows he may have something to do with an outfit, now defunct, known as the European Security Office."

The blonde Scavenger nodded. "What has he learned about Dr. Hawksworth?"

Walpole licked at his dry lips before replying. "He knows she probably had something to do with his past. That, though, was half a blooming century ago."

The bentwood rocker stopped rocking. "You, Mr. Walpole, know more about him than he does, don't you?"

"How could that be, old boy? I meant to say, it's his

bloody quest now, isn't it?"

"Mr. Walpole, Mr. Walpole, you forget we already know."

"Then why make me say it again?"

"I've already explained."

Walpole said, "What are you Scavengers up to? I mean, what blooming difference does it make to you what makes Gypsy tick?"

"The Scavengers," explained the plump young man, who'd resumed his slow, steady rocking, "are dedicated to improving the world, Mr. Walpole, to fixing it up."

"You've not done a smashing job so far," Walpole told him. "Some of your decor ain't bad, but your manners could stand a bit of improving. Especially when it comes to kicking a chap when he's down."

"The world, especially a world in the shabby shape ours is, doesn't always cooperate with an organization like the Scavengers. Therefore, we have to use force."

"I got you pegged now," said Walpole. "One of those perishing rule-the-world gangs." He laughed. "Not much of a ruddy world left to rule."

"It will be improved, Mr. Walpole. Once all the fragments have been pulled together. Then we'll have a world empire, smoothly run and efficient."

"And belonging to the Scavengers."

"Yes, exactly."

Walpole laughed some more. "You're like those historical blokes I've heard about," he said. "Had a pal once who was a computer, Fax was his name, and he filled me in on some of them. Lads like Caesar and Alexander and that Hitler. Didn't work out for any of them."

"None of them had the organization the Scavengers have, Mr. Walpole, nor anything like our dedication."

"Tell us the rest of what you know about Gypsy," the big man ordered. "The part he doesn't know himself."

EIGHT

The blind man fell out of the blimp. He dropped to the dusty landing field, a fall of a little over five feet, hit the ground on his left side, sent up a swirl of pale yellow dust, and rolled until he hit against the legs of a Black baggage attendant. "Missed the blasted offramp," he explained as the attendant picked him up.

"Cheer up, Señor, once you visit the Shrine of Saint Skippy you'll see with the keenness of a hawk."

"Are hawks noted for their eyesight?" The blind man was kicking at the ground, in hopes of locating his cane.

Up at the disembark door of the pilgrim blimp a stewardess was helping a one-legged Chinese man onto the ramp. "Don't take a dive like that last guy," she cautioned.

"Not old Bob Foo," the Chinese assured her. "I'm nimble, and when old Saint Skippy grows me a new leg you're really going to see old Bob Foo cut some capers . . . oops!"

"Pull your crutch ferrule out of that ramp rut, Mr. Foo."

"Okay now, Bob Foo is all set."

Gypsy and Annabelle were next in line.

The stewardess observed, "You don't seem feeble and infirm at all."

"We," Annabelle informed her, "simply wish the experience of visiting the shrine."

"You'll sure get that," said the stewardess. "I've been out there several times, mainly because there isn't much else to do in the Cape Verde Islands, and I always come away feeling very spiritual. Once he even cleared up a wart I used to have right here."

"Let's hurry right out there," Gypsy said, taking Annabelle's arm and guiding her down to the ground from the slightly swaying blimp.

It was a warm, muggy afternoon on São Tiago. The

palm trees surrounding the blimp field looked soggy, the rocky landscape was blurred.

"I wish we'd picked another way to get here," said Annabelle. "Pretending to be pilgrims is starting to be a strain."

"Easiest way to get here," said Gypsy as they walked away from the unloading blimp. "And it gives us a good excuse to be here."

"Yeah, but now we have to traipse out to this silly shrine and—"

"Relics, Señora? Would you and your handsome husband like a souvenir of the blessed Saint Skippy?" A bent and twisted woman in a tattered coverall had approached them. She hobbled alongside Gypsy. "I have shirt sleeves, collars, a nice assortment of buttons, some neckerchiefs, a straw hat, two umbrellas, a swatch of—"

"No, thanks," said Annabelle.

"How about a pair of his old socks? I have argyles, knits, neosilk, and, at a dearer price, one dayglo sock with a picture of a clock on it." She shook the wicker basket slung around her neck.

"We'll wait until we reach the actual shrine."

"Ah, but if you buy from Saint Skippy himself, you won't get bargain prices like these."

Gypsy shook his head, and the vending woman stopped following them.

"She assumed we were a married couple," said the girl.

"Good. It makes us look even less suspicious."

They'd reached a wide street; white stone buildings with tile roofs came into view.

Making a face, Annabelle said, "You're not even sure Walpole is being held on this particular island. There are nine or ten of them, after all."

"I feel he is. That's all I can tell you."

"Can you come up with a few more hunches for us? Like a nice address? Save us a lot of legwork."

Gypsy grinned. "It may be that my abilities, even when I'm in complete control, aren't that efficient."

"You still believe that damn vulture wasn't conning you?"

"We wouldn't have made this pilgrimage if—"

"Yow!" A portly Black man in a white two-piece pilgrim suit had suddenly fallen flat on his face a few yards directly ahead of them on the hot sidewalk.

Gypsy ran up to him. "What's wrong?"

"I knew I should have dumped more in the collection plate," he said, panting.

Helping him to a sitting position, Gypsy asked, "Have you had some sort of fit?"

"My 'miracle' ran out," replied the Black man. "I was out at the shrine this morning and Saint Skippy cured my arthritis. Thing is, I only dropped fifty smackers in the plate—a wicker serving dish, actually—when his sexton passed it around. Should have made it a couple hundred, I guess. I was strolling along, enjoying my new mobility, when—whammo! I'm gimpy all over again."

"Where are you staying?" Annabelle asked him. "We can haul you there."

"Down the street, young lady, at the Cabeza Doida Hotel."

"So are we."

"You'll be doing me a real favor, helping me home." When he was back on his feet, he added, "My name is Mel Furioso, from Ngumi over in Africa. This is my second pilgrimage to the Cape Verdes. Saint Skippy has really made a believer of me."

"Too bad," observed Annabelle, "that his 'miracles' don't last a bit longer."

"My own darn fault," said Furioso.

While they helped him hobble to the hotel, Gypsy asked, "Many other things to see on this island?"

"Well, you might like to visit the monastery. Call themselves the São Tiago Brotherhood and produce all the coffee grown on this island nowadays." He wiped at his face with a white handkerchief. "An unfriendly bunch, if you ask me. I get the idea they're sort of mean as well."

"Mean. How so?"

"On my way out to the shrine this morning my driver took a wrong turn. We wound up on some back road behind the coffee fields, must have been about seven this morning," related Furioso. "All at once a tall, skinny young fellow in nothing but his underwear came running out from amongst the coffee plants and onto the road. Before I could even tell my landcar driver to stop, three or four of the Brothers showed up and grabbed him. They knocked him around, then dragged him back onto the plantation. I asked my driver about it and he says, 'Only a novice, Señor, who's had second thoughts about joining the order.' "

"Tall and lean guy, you say?" asked Gypsy.

"Tall, skinny, somewhere in his middle twenties, I'd estimate."

After a glance at Annabelle, Gypsy said, "What other things ought we to see on São Tiago?"

Annabelle took one more sip of her punch. She placed her glass on the tiletop table, leaned back, and watched the approaching Gypsy.

He came striding across the hotel terrace. "Hello, sweetheart," he said as he sat down opposite her.

"Just part of the masquerade, isn't it? These fond terms."

"Obviously," he said, grinning.

Annabelle nodded. There were several other hotel guests scattered at the dozen outdoor tables. "This island doesn't seem to have fallen apart quite as badly as some parts of the world."

"Out here in the Atlantic, it wasn't touched very much by what happened in Europe or even across there in Africa," said Gypsy. "And ever since Saint Skippy saw his vision twenty-seven years ago, the pilgrimage business has made São Tiago relatively affluent."

"Did you find out anything else, besides the state of the island's finances?"

He frowned, watching her pretty face. "You're a little feisty, Annabelle."

"Oh, am I? I don't know why I should be, sitting on my duff all afternoon and then when you finally show up and say one lousy nice thing to me you tell me it's only part of your damn disguise."

Gypsy considered replying to that, then didn't. After a moment, he said, "There's a strong possibility the São Tiago Brotherhood boys' monastery and plantation is a cover for a Scavenger headquarters."

"La-di-da," muttered the girl into her glass.

"What?"

Straightening up, Annabelle said, "Nothing, chief. Excuse it. Back to business and all that."

"I've been asking questions casually," said Gypsy. "Talked to merchants, shopkeepers, hotel people, posing as a nosy tourist who's interested in worthwhile places to take his charming wife while on São Tiago. I've found out there are roughly twenty-five members of the order, plus some fifty coffee plantation workers. Ten or so of the plantation employees live right at the monastery along with the Brothers—they're guys who act as guards and so on. The monastery, however, buys enough food, wine, and other supplies to feed at least twice as many

people as are supposedly living there."

"Could be they're all gluttons."

"A possibility, but a likelier one is that there are more people out at that place than is immediately evident," he said. "There used to be an underground system of tombs beneath the chapel at the monastery. Be a good spot for a concealed headquarters operation."

"If the Brothers are openly buying up all these supplies, isn't that too obvious? I mean, doesn't that make everyone suspicious?"

Gypsy said, "The goods are purchased from a number of merchants, some of whom are rivals. They don't get together and compare notes. Besides, Annabelle, there isn't any worldwide police organization. Nobody's hunting for the Scavengers except us, far as I'm aware. So they have to be careful, but not that elaborately."

"Any further hints about Walpole? Could he have been the one Mr. Furioso came across this morning?"

"No one else remembers seeing anyone resembling Walpole, out at the monastery or anywhere on São Tiago," he answered.

"So what next?"

"We find out if Walpole *is* there," said Gypsy. "If he is, we get him out."

The rusted skeleton of the Golden Gate Bridge, broken and lying scattered in the muddy waters of San Francisco Bay, was visible from the curved one-way windows of the tower. The tower itself rose above the collapsed Victorian houses scattered across the steep hillside. About a hundred yards downhill from the tower a jagged gully sliced the street in half, a reminder of the Big Quake. Weeds and high grass grew in the chasm now.

The woman who stood at the tower window watching the distant bay was tall, six feet at least, and thin. Dark, thirty-one, gauntly attractive. She wore grey trousers, black realleather boots, and a grey sleeveless tunic. "We just about have him," she said.

A hefty perspiring man sat in a tin chair, his back to the view. "If Furioso is to be believed," he said.

Jackita Teal remained at the windows. The blue of the late afternoon sky was commencing, gradually, to thin. "He's reliable, Pres."

"Anybody with a pseudonym like that," said Preston Bookings, "I'd be very careful with."

"Furioso is his *real* name," Jackita said. "You ought to read the membership dossiers with more care."

"We've machines to do that." From a flap pocket of his three-piece loungesuit he took a kerchief to wipe at his broad face. "Do you really think we're completely ready to move in on Gypsy?"

"Very nearly," she replied.

"We ought to wait. I'm fearful of another Wondersmith fiasco." The perspiration reappeared on Bookings' ruddy face. "He was a very bright man who—"

"He was a very bright *old* man," corrected Jackita. "Old and stubborn, not worth the trouble of converting and certainly not someone who could be bribed into working for me."

"*You*? Are you and the Scavengers one and the same now?"

"A slip, Pres, forgive me," she said, smiling faintly, although not at him. "Even though I'm the head of the world organization, I realize the Scavengers is a cooperative effort."

"*Do* you, now?" he rubbed away the sweat once again. "Well, let us get back to the Gypsy matter if we may. We simply don't know enough about him yet. We ought to wait."

"*Wait*? Wait and allow him to break into one of our headquarters complexes?"

"Give him his friend back—that young man is of no use to us."

"No, Pres," said the lean Jackita. "We have Gypsy just about to walk right into our parlor. We'll grab him when he does."

"You mean we'll *try*."

"And *succeed*. What's being set up to welcome Gypsy, Pres . . . he's not going to get out of that." She abandoned the bay and turned to stare at the sweating man. "He's going to be matched against three of the most sophisticated weapons the Scavengers have on hand. We'll stop him—and hold onto him."

"Perhaps," said Bookings. He plucked at the portions of his suit which were clinging to his perspiring body. "It's possible Gypsy will beat our weapons. Or they may kill him. Either way, what'll we have?"

"No one wants him dead—he's worth much too much. He's to be *captured* on São Tiago, not killed."

"Without bringing up Wondersmith again, I don't have as much faith in some of our field people as you do."

Jackita said, "Once we have Gypsy . . ." She ceased speaking, a thin smile touching her lean face.

"We really don't know enough about him."

"But we *do*, Pres. We know exactly what he was intended to be. That's why I want him in the Scavenger arsenal."

"We know *something* about what Gypsy was intended to be," he reminded her. "Not all—and we still have only a vague idea of his powers. He may well be capable of many more—"

"We're going to move against him now." She crossed the circular room to a wide metal desk. Resting a narrow hip against it, she said, "We know considerably more about Gypsy than he does."

"*That's* not a major achievement, since the poor fellow is an amnesiac for all practical purposes."

"But we have those journals of Dr. Hawksworth," said the Scavenger leader. "They give us a great deal of background on Gypsy, on the whole project. We may not be aware of all the abilities Hawksworth and her crew gave him, granted. But we do know pretty well what they had in mind for him—and for the others that were to come after."

"Yes, I realize that," said Bookings. "Putting that information together with what we obtained from Walpole . . . well, it does fill in some gaps—especially when you consider his background, in ways which frankly unsettle me. Realizing what this Gypsy was before . . . I don't know. Even if we can get him to work with us, he may well be too dangerous."

"What he was, what he did . . . that's all buried in the last century," said Jakita. "The important thing is what Gypsy is *now*. *That* we can use."

More memories.

Sitting alone on the balcony of his hotel room, eyes absently turned toward the midnight sky, Gypsy remembered.

Not the white room this time. No figures circling him, staring down at him.

There were people, hundreds of them. People from *then*, dressed in the clothes of a half-century ago.

And lights. Lights, hot and glaring, floating in the black of the night. Exploding yellow. Flashing red. All blurring and blending into one vast throbbing, spinning glare.

Running.

The crowd shouting, crying out, cursing.

"That's him! There he goes!"

"Get him! Grab him! Stop him!"

"The bastard, the dirty bastard!"

"Get him!"

Stumbling—and the hands got him. Hundreds of hands. They punched him, clawed him, tore at him, ripped his clothes, his flesh.

Gypsy suddenly rubbed at his synthetic arm.

The memory was lost.

He couldn't remember where he had been, why the crowd had been after him, dogging him.

And when had it happened? Back *then*, obviously, back in the twentieth century. But had it been before, or after . . .

No more of that sentence. Before or after *what*?

Still rubbing at the false arm, fingers rasping the imitation skin, Gypsy strained to recall.

He couldn't.

Expelling his breath, he sank back in the sling chair.

A new image inside his head. Something he hadn't remembered at all before.

Sunlight, and quiet. A high narrow rectangle of brightness. Curtains, pale yellow, fluttering very slightly. Outside there were fields. Brown earth, rows of trees. Fruit trees. An orchard.

He couldn't go out there.

Why? Why couldn't he?

He couldn't move at all.

No, that wasn't quite right. Gypsy could move his head. He could turn, gaze out that single tall window at the orchards beyond.

Beyond where?

A cottage. Yes, a stone cottage. It was in an agricultural community. A small community which had survived, and it was somewhere in . . . in France.

Sure, because Dr. Emerson had told him. Emerson talked to him all the time as he worked.

Sitting there in the darkness, in 2033, his hand rubbing and rubbing at his arm, Gypsy struggled with his memory. He had remembered a name: Dr. Emerson. But he had no idea who the man was.

Emerson worked with Dr. Hawksworth, didn't he?

Did he?

He was a middle-aged man, medium-sized, smiling and grinning all the time no matter what was going on. Dark curly hair and a black beard . . . no, not black. White. His hair and beard were white, his face brown and scribbled with wrinkles. An old man.

Two images of Emerson. Young, old. Mixed.

"I must have known him for a long time. Back then I knew him and later . . . Paris! We had to go to Paris for some reason. We had to—"

"Gypsy? What's wrong?"

He jumped from his chair, spun. "What?"

"You were moaning," said Annabelle as she took a tentative step out onto the small balcony. "I came over from my room to see you and when you didn't answer, I let myself in."

"I remember locking my door."

"You forget I have a knack for getting into places," she said. "A holdover from my flaming youth. Are you okay?"

Very slowly, he nodded his head. "I've been remembering things, about myself."

"The process doesn't seem to have cheered you up."

"No, not much."

Moving nearer to him, the dark-haired girl said, "This might be a good time to stop digging into yourself, Gypsy. We'll pull Walpole out of this tight place, then—"

"There's a lot more back there in the twentieth century," he told her "Something I did, something that turned people against me . . . it's all tied in with what I am now."

"Chinese puzzle," said Annabelle.

"What?"

"I remember hearing about a Chinese puzzle box. You open one box and there's another inside it, and you open that and there's another box inside it. Hate to think of your life being nothing but opening boxes."

"There's no way around . . . hold on." He crossed swiftly and silently to the balcony rail. After looking down at the late-night street for a few seconds, he came back to Annabelle. "Going to take a stroll. You wait here."

"Stroll? What's down there?"

"Our friend Furioso," replied Gypsy. "I've been waiting for him to go out."

"What made you think he would?"

"He might want to report to someone."

"Report what?"

"That we seem to have taken the bait."

TEN

The leaves rattled in the night wind, shadow patterns formed and reformed on the moonlit trail. Gypsy traveled parallel to the narrow pathway, remaining hidden among the dark trees.

Furioso was a hundred yards ahead of him, walking briskly. He had not hired a cab, but had come out in the direction of the São Tiago Brotherhood monastery and plantation on foot. He exhibited none of his earlier difficulty in walking—being unaware, Gypsy was certain, that he was being followed.

A night bird called, the leaves rustled.

Another half-mile and the forest began to thin. A wide roadway with a low rock wall on its far side loomed up. This was the back side of the coffee plantation.

The plump Black man crossed the road.

The more Gypsy had thought about Furioso, the less he had trusted him. He'd dropped too conveniently into their path, and his story about seeing Walpole trying to escape from the monastery wasn't quite convincing. An organization as efficient as Gypsy assumed the Scavengers was didn't let people escape, didn't chase out after them in the open in broad daylight. And even if they had, they'd have made damned sure Furioso and his driver didn't get away to tell about it.

Which all indicated they'd been expecting Gypsy to come to this island to look for his friend. Furioso had fed him a story which would make him come nosing around the monastery, and then a trap would be sprung. Gypsy figured by trailing the Black man, by approaching the hangout when he might not be expected, he'd be able to locate Walpole.

Furioso had halted, was seating himself on the rock wall. Probably waiting for someone to meet him.

A night bird called and called and called. The shrill, piercing sound seemed to fill Gypsy's skull. It wasn't a

bird at all, it was some sort of mechanical wail.

Wailing not outside in the night, but inside his head. Corkscrewing into his brain.

Gypsy brought his hands up to his temples. He bent, rocking slightly. At first he was aware of nothing but that wailing. Then, as the sound diminished, he heard voices. People shouting, feet pounding on pavement.

"There he is! There he is!"

"Get the bastard!"

"Did he really do it?"

Straightening, pain still spinning around inside him, Gypsy saw the crowd. Hundreds of people, men and women, all dressed in the clothes of that fifty-years-ago time.

They filled the road, and the road was no longer a dirt road. It was made of bright translucent plastic, orange-tinted. The plantation was still there, except that some buildings had cropped up among the coffee bushes. Buildings he almost remembered.

The crowd was aware of Gypsy. They were pointing, shouting, waving fists as they commenced stalking him slowly.

"Get him! Get him!"

"Trample him!"

"Tear him apart!"

They were running, running along the plastic walk-ramp. And yet somehow raising dust.

Gypsy started to run, too. He zigzagged across the road, jumped over a low rock wall, and was onto the plantation grounds.

"Bravo! Bravo!" Furioso was applauding him. "Damn good show!" He'd changed his clothes, was wearing a tuxedo. Something from the last century. "Don't let them get you down, Gypsy, old man!"

That was encouraging, someone on his side.

Gypsy had to stop, because there was a high reviewing stand in front of him. Deserted, chairs knocked over, but . . . there was someone up there.

One man, slumped over the wooden railing, arm dangling, white-blonde head ruined. There was hardly half a skull top. The rest of it had been shot away. Its contents were splashed on the planking of the stand and were now leaking down across the red, white, and blue bunting.

"It's him! He's over there!"

"Grab him! Stop him!"

"You can't get away with this!"

They were coming for him, stomping through the rows of coffee bushes, racing along curving pedways, screaming, shouting, warning him of what they meant to do.

"Gypsy, run!" urged Furioso, who was sitting on the reviewing stand in a folding chair, a pair of opera glasses resting on one plump knee. "Don't let them catch you."

Gypsy started running again. It was getting more and more difficult, he was growing incredibly tired.

"Defense #301."

Gypsy stumbled through the bushes, stumbling, staggering.

"Defense #301."

Who was saying that? Why didn't they quit, stop bothering him.

"Defense #301." There he was. A medium-sized bearded man, resting in a comfortable armchair next to a flowering coffee bush. His hair color was fading, going from black to white. "Defense #301, remember?"

Gypsy slowed up, halted. He did remember.

The crowd was coming closer.

He narrowed his eyes, pressed his palms together. Inside his head he could almost feel a sudden snapping. He'd been able to utilize his defense against the hallucination beam they'd obviously been using on him.

There was silence now. The hundreds had vanished, the reviewing stand and the dead man were gone. Old Dr. Emerson as well.

Gypsy scanned the field. Even Furioso was gone—and he'd been real. Everything else had come out of Gypsy's mind, stimulated by whatever hallucinogenic gadget they'd tried against him. Used to first disorient and then disable him.

But he'd remembered defense #301.

Had he? Even now Gypsy wasn't exactly sure what he'd done. Some sort of mental exercise which had stopped the hallucinations.

Moving forward, Gypsy shook his head. He'd found out something more about himself, but—

The ground opened beneath him and he went plunging down. Down and down a winding metal tunnel.

He rolled and tumbled, sliding downward into darkness, elbows and knees banging at the metal walls.

Then a long drop through chilled air.

Gypsy hit bottom, landing on his side, a stone floor. Light flared all around him. Thin strips of harsh yellow light ringing the walls of the circular room. A large room with six open doorways cutting into it.

He was getting to his feet when something came whistling at him from above.

A small silvery object, like half an orange in size and shape. It circled his head twice, very fast, then smacked against the back of his neck.

The impact was such, surprisingly, that Gypsy went tottering forward. The thing was attached to his flesh, was sinking long, rasping metallic tendrils into his neck.

He reached around with his left hand, his good hand, to grasp at the mechanical parasite.

"Yow!"

A terrific electric shock went shooting into his fingers the instant he touched the thing.

Gypsy tried to grab it with his right hand. Again a severe shock.

He could feel the tendrils of the parasite burrowing into him. Seeking out his spine, his brain.

Spinning, Gypsy threw himself back against the nearest metal wall. He might be able to dislodge the damned thing that way.

He wasn't successful.

The parasite hung on.

And a voice commenced speaking to Gypsy, from inside his head.

"Numbered doors," the voice said, a dim faraway voice without gender or emotion. "Do you see?"

Gypsy attempted another swat at the thing, received another shock.

"Numbered doors. Look."

Pain began filling his head, forcing him to look around at the doors.

"Do you see?" asked the voice inside him.

"Yes," he found himself replying.

"Door 6. Where is it?"

"Yeah, I see it."

"Point to it."

More pain, new and different, knifing into his spine.

Gypsy managed to lift his hand to point at the door with the number 6 stenciled over it. "There."

"You will enter that doorway," he was instructed. "You will walk along the corridor beyond."

Fists clenched, Gypsy did not comply.

"You will walk along that corridor."

The pain this time grabbed him around his middle, making him double up and groan.

"You will walk along the corridor," repeated the voice.

Somewhere in his memory another voice was talking, trying to reach him. ". . . do . . . such circumstances . . ."

"Walk," ordered the pain-inducing voice.

"Attempted parasite control," the other voice, the voice trapped and lost in Gypsy's memory years ago, was saying. "Follow standard repel procedures."

Gypsy struggled to stand erect, fought to think. To remember what he had to do.

"Use telek powers whenever possible."

That's right. All he had to do was—

The pain filled him up, twisted his insides, scraped his skull, raked at his nerves.

Gypsy held out. Crouched, hugging himself, he fought against the pain and the parasite control device which had attached itself to him.

He had to concentrate, work against the damned thing.

He had to cause it to . . .

Gypsy stayed huddled several seconds before he realized the source of the pain was gone and he was feeling only its diminishing echoes.

The Scavengers had tried to use a control gadget on him, but he'd remembered what to do. The standard procedures which . . . who? He couldn't exactly recollect. Whose voice had come back to him explaining what must be done? Dr. Hawksworth's? Dr. Emerson's?

Hadn't been a woman's voice. Meaning . . .

"Door 3."

A perception: to reach Walpole he had to travel along corridor 3. He crossed to the doorway out.

"You ain't much in the way of company," Walpole observed from the wooden chair that he had leaned against the stone wall of his cell.

"No frills," replied the large android which stood near the door. "Built to kill, to administer brutal punishment. No small talk."

"Don't apologize, old top. Now that I reflect, I've shared cells with worse." He kept a steady watch on the giant mechanical man.

The fellow was well over seven feet tall, built to resemble a weightlifter, broad and blonde, wearing a one-piece plyo fightsuit.

Walpole ran his tongue along a crack in his upper left canine tooth—a crack he'd acquired since coming to the Scavenger stronghold. "We been bunk mates for near a whole bloody day now," he said to the muscular mechanism. "Whyn't you break down and tell me why you're here?"

"Stomp somebody."

"Me, do you mean?"

"Small potatoes."

"Am I? So who's the target then, mate?"

"Visitor."

"I ain't expecting any perishing company."

"Probably not," acknowledged the android. "If bandana man get by other two devices, then there is me."

"Bandana man—" Walpole let his chair swing forward until the front legs touched the stone floor. "Would you, old boy, be expecting a chap by the name of Gypsy?"

"*Gypsy*, yes. Going to work on him."

Walpole said, "You mean these bloody Scavengers are going to kill Gypsy?"

"Not kill—catch and subdue."

"Oh, yes? So they can find out what makes him tick?"

"He's important. Useful."

"I doubt whether Gypsy'll be much use to you balmy idiots."

"Force him."

"*Will* you, now?"

"Very strong," explained the huge android. "Crush anything, anybody."

"I'll place my quid on Gypsy."

"Means what?"

"Skip it, mate. I don't fancy they programmed you to bet."

"No record of such."

"Thought not." Casually, Walpole got out of his chair. "Why'd you drop in today? They expecting Gypsy?"

"Already here."

Grinning, Walpole said, "He *is*? Warms me cockles! If Gyp's nearby, then I should soon—"

"Not likely to reach us. Prepared if he does."

"I fancy he . . . ah, good to see you again, gov."

Gypsy had materialized in the exact center of the cell.

"Fight now," announced the large android as it turned

toward him. "Subdue you."

Moving to his friend's side, Gypsy said, "I seem to be getting control of myself. Let's go."

"Ain't you to tussle with this bloke? Show him who's who and give him what-for?"

"It's not necessary." Gypsy took hold of Walpole's arm.

Then they were gone from the underground room.

"Not fair," complained the enormous android.

Welcome To Ophir!

The words glowed over the arched stone gateway to the walled African city.

Another Fabled Lost City To Serve You!

Walpole was dragging his feet on the twilight roadway, kicking up tiny swirls of yellow dust. "I don't like the feel of this bleeding place."

"It's better than captivity," pointed out Annabelle, who was walking between him and Gypsy.

"That remains to be established." The lean Englishman eyed a lion who was coming down the steps of a souvenir shop.

"What I mean is," persisted the girl, "it'll be pleasanter than being a prisoner of the Scavengers."

"Don't go riding that blooming hobbyhorse again, lass." The lion was sniffing at Walpole's hand, tail swishing. "I thought Ophir was supposed to be a tourist town. Wild beasts slobbering on a bloke ain't me idea of a tourist attraction."

Gypsy said, "The lion's mechanical."

"Is it now, gov?" Walpole halted to study the beast. "Coulda fooled me. How can you tell?"

"I can tell."

"*Nice* machine," said Walpole, extending his hand, very tentatively, toward the robot lion's mane. "Go off and stalk somebody else, whyn't you?"

"You were," said Annabelle when they resumed walking and left the lion standing there, "a prisoner of the Scavengers, weren't you? Not simply a house guest?"

"We had this all out on the bloody tourist boat coming over here, pet."

"Sometimes I tend to harp on things," admitted Annabelle. "If you insist you aren't on chummy terms with the Scavenger crowd—well, I have to believe you, I suppose."

"Listen now." Walpole's head tilted close to hers. "Those barmy bastards worked me over for—"

"Hey, enough squabbling," put in Gypsy as he took each of them by the arm. "We're here in Ophir for a reason."

"*You're* here for a reason," amended Walpole. "That don't mean we had to drag this unbelieving wench along to—"

"No great help you are, either," said the girl. "Falling into traps, getting yourself kidnapped, wandering off . . . why did you ditch us back at Gibraltar?"

"Maybe to get away from shrewish tongues, lass." He glanced at Gypsy. "Anyways, I've told the gov here I'll explain all that shortly."

"As soon," said Annabelle, "as you think up a good excuse for deserting."

"Get something straight in your coco, you twittering idiot. I didn't desert Gypsy. He went off on his perishing quest, left us parked on that rock with a bunch of agricultural sods and a gaggle of robot monkeys who—"

"King Solomon's Mines! King Solomon's Mines! Don't miss 'em!" A seven-foot-tall Black man, clad in a leopard skin and many bright beads, was beckoning from a light-trimmed doorway.

"Didn't realize the perishing things was so easy to come by."

"First expedition for the fabled treasure hordes now departing! Two flights down . . . only twenty-five dollars! King Solomon's Mines! King Solomon's Mines!"

"I'm surprised a town like this can thrive," remarked Annabelle as they continued down the main street of Ophir.

Gypsy had been scanning the fairly crowded walk-ways, the multinational tourists, the bright buildings and shops offering all the excitement and treasures of a long-vanished and considerably mythical Africa. "Quite a few countries are still functioning," he said. "Enough to provide tourists and vacationers for places such as Ophir."

"Good thing, too," said Walpole. "It'll help us in our masquerade. Otherwise . . . oops!"

An extremely muscular man in a loincloth had gone swinging overhead on a vine, his bare feet nearly clunking Walpole's shaggy head.

"Lord of the Jungle Café! Lord of the Jungle Café!" shouted the barker in front of the stone building the loinclothed man had swung into. "Gourmet cooking! Jungle ambience! Presided over by a gent rumored to have been raised by apes!"

"I wouldn't go bragging about nothing like that," said Walpole, "by some of the apes *I've* met."

"There's the office we want." Annabelle tugged at Gypsy's sleeve, pointing to a glowing sign across the darkening street.

The sign announced *Quatermain, Inc. Authentic Safaris Into The Jungles And Velds Of Africa!*

"We'll join up." Gypsy went striding toward the safari office.

Walpole swatted at another one. "Ow!" He separated his palms and examined the remains of the mosquito. "Wires and circuits. Blimey!"

"All part of the African atmosphere." Gypsy was seated in a rattan chair on the terrace of their suite at the Jewels of Opar Hotel. "Want to talk now?"

After blowing the wreckage of the robot insect into a nearby flowering bush, the lanky young man paced a few paces across the flagstones. He turned his back to Gypsy, watching the darkness and the distant lights of the town.

"Didn't want the lass in on this chat, gov," he said after a moment. "Let me ask you first off . . . you're going to stick with this perishing quest of yours, ain't you?"

"I have to. It's the only way, as I told you, that I can find out who I am."

"You was saying earlier, gov, as how there are some fairly decent spots still operating in this bunged-up world." Slowly Walpole faced his friend. "You could settle in one of them, earn a soft living with all the exceptional talents you got, and—"

"There are several reasons why I can't," Gypsy interrupted. "Not the least of which is tied to what just happened at the plantation. The records I was able to dig up in Villedeux indicated that the next stop in this game I'm supposed to be playing is to be here in Africa. In a place now called Ngumi, roughly a hundred miles south of here."

"I know, I know, gov, you filled me in during our blinking boat ride from the Cape Verdes," said Walpole. "The thing is, old top, this blooming game was set up fifty years ago. I mean to say, there ain't many folks left who give a damn about the outcome. Be the same if it was a cricket match, don't you know. Nobody's going to sit around for a blessed half a century to—"

"Nobody needed to play a cricket game to find out where they came from—to discover who they used to be," reminded Gypsy. As the light from the glass door of the suite did not quite touch him, he sat in darkness. "Another consideration is the Scavengers."

"Aw, a bunch of blooming fanatics. Power-goofy, like them Queen Bess wenches we tangled with back home in—"

"The Scavengers are considerably more dangerous. And they *know* about *me*."

"Got to admit they do," said Walpole, slouching,

thrusting his hands into his pockets. "Them blokes'd like to add you to their list."

"Okay, so in order to keep that from happening I have to know more about myself," Gypsy told his friend.

"I don't think they're going to be any too anxious about making another try to recruit you. Not after the demonstration you gave them over in São Tiago."

"I'm still not sure of my abilities, though."

"You used them pretty well."

"Still, I was afraid to teleport us over here to the African coast."

"The boat trip wasn't all that bad."

"Even if the Scavengers leave me alone, they're going to keep on collecting weapons," said Gypsy. "I want to stop that, and prevent them from murdering any more people like Wondersmith."

"Live and let live," suggested Walpole. "We don't have to go poking—"

"*I* do."

Walpole lowered himself into a sling chair. "I suppose you're right, gov," he said. "In a way, I wouldn't mind booby-trapping them Scavenger blokes. But since I learned a bit about life whilst maturing in the sleazier sections of Merry Olde England, I sort of believe running in an opposite direction from trouble ain't a half-bad code to live by."

Gypsy moved slightly, and the light slanting out of the suite touched at his face. "Is that why you left Gibraltar?"

Walpole devoted the next fifty or so seconds to clearing his throat. "Well, the Scavengers had a bit to do with my ending up where you found me, gov."

"You were running away *before* they grabbed you."

"True," admitted Walpole. "Let's see, can I come up with an explanation of *that*."

"There's nothing about myself that I'm afraid to hear," Gypsy said. "You found out something about me, when we were going through the archives in Spain."

"You been listening to them nasty rumors Annabelle gives out about me, gov," said Walpole. "Which ain't to say they're not true." He let out his breath and rubbed his bony hands together. "Well now, I did happen to read some info concerning you, gov. Stuff I thought you might . . . you'd best not hear right off."

"I'd like to hear it now."

Walpole's head lowered. He seemed very interested in what his hands were doing to each other. "Okay," he said.

THIRTEEN

Three leopards lolled in the sunny morning street near the hotel entrance. A chimpanzee hunkered near them, chattering, grimacing.

"They're going to devour us," said a plump woman tourist from Germany 3.

"Nonsense, Helga," her plump husband assured her. "They're all robots."

"Oh? Then how come I saw that chimp do his business not two minutes ago?"

"A very sophisticated robot can do anything."

"Grim," Annabelle was saying to Gypsy, her hand on his arm as they walked toward the center of Ophir. "You seem very grim today."

"I'm fine," Gypsy said. "Looking forward to our safari, even if it is only an excuse to get unobtrusively close to Ngumi."

"Come on, I know you," said the girl. And you're much different than you were last night. Did Walpole tell you something negative?"

Gypsy replied, "He told me what he'd been keeping back."

"Which is why you're downcast this morning."

"I'm thoughtful."

Several Foreign Legionnaire androids went marching by, gear rattling.

"Then," persisted Annabelle, "he *did* tell you something about yourself?"

"Yes, that's right."

"Well, what?"

"Don't worry, I'll tell you. But not right yet. I want to—"

"Brood. You want to brood some more, suffer in silence. Honestly, Gypsy, you—"

"After I get to Ngumi, and locate the European Security facility, the remains of it . . . I should know

more about why I am what I am," he said. "And possibly
the challenge they set up may still be operative. Sometimes I can get a clue from—"

"Whoa, now," cut in the girl. "Did you say after *you*
get to Ngumi?"

"It might be better if you and Walpole—"

"Nix." Annabelle shook her head violently. "How
many times, good heavens, do I have to remind you we're
a team! A team, Gypsy dear, consists of more than *one*
member. Traditionally."

He nodded briefly, didn't reply, and they continued
along toward the safari offices in silence.

A block from the business premises of Quatermain,
Inc., from the alley next to the café which boasted an entire staff made up of chimpanzees, a cluster of people
came tumbling out accompanied by barking dogs. Dust
whirled up from the street, dogs snarled, a half-dozen or
more burly men were cursing and swinging their fists.

From the core of the tussle came a familiar voice.
"Half a mo, you blokes. What say we make this a fair
go? Three to one instead of seven."

As Annabelle cried, "They've got Walpole!" Gypsy
went running for the group.

They were big men, bearded, clad in bright robes and
headcloths.

A shopkeeper, lingering in the doorway of his pseudo-
ivory shop, advised the charging Gypsy, "It's only pickpockets at work, sir. They won't kill him."

Ignoring him, Gypsy caught the shoulders of the nearest and, coincidently, biggest pickpocket and lifted him
clean of the fight. Grunting very slightly, Gypsy flung the
big man aside.

"Aiiiy, a thousand curses on your bandannaed head!"
howled the man immediately before smacking into a neo-
marble table at the adjacent outdoor café. The table legs

gave in, tipping him smack into a tuxedoed chimpanzee.

By this time Gypsy was flinging another pickpocket. "Off, leave him be!"

This one got a cartwheeling motion going, ending up clear across the street in a loincloth boutique's outdoor display bin.

The third thug spun to snarl at Gypsy. "What's the big idea of interfering with a man at his work?"

"Go away," suggested Gypsy. He aided the process.

The man, dancing backward, returned rapidly into the alley, fell over one of the dogs, and made a yellow-and-red-striped bundle where he sank.

"I'm commencing to see daylight." Walpole was flat on his back, with three of the pickpockets working him over with fist and foot. He managed to buckle his knees and kick out, sending one of his bulky assailants flying into the pickpocket Gypsy had just sent spinning off.

"Save one of the remaining ones for me, gov." Pressing his right hand against the dusty ground and using his arm as a lever, he pushed himself upright.

The two remaining thugs didn't wait to be divided and shared. Gathering the frayed skirts of their colorful robes, they went scurrying away down the alley. The pack of dogs followed, yelping.

"One of the inevitable blights of any tourist town, sir," observed the shopkeeper from the doorway.

"The only trouble with fighting whilst flat on one's arse," remarked Walpole while he dusted himself off, "is it's a bit mucky."

"How'd you come to tangle with them?"

"One of the blighters made a grab for me wallet." Walpole wiped at his dirt-streaked forehead with the heel of his hand. "As he weren't very deft, I noticed what he was about. When I grabbed his mitt in the act, the rest of them hopped atop me."

"I hear they don't go in for killing."

"Oh, so?" With one booted foot Walpole poked at the long-bladed knife lying in the gutter. "That weren't the bloody impression the lad toting that there give me."

"They seldom," said the shopkeeper, "commit murder, sir."

"Seldom ain't never."

Annabelle ran over to them. "You've got to stop rubbing people the wrong way, Walpole. You all right?"

"Takes more than seven surly bad'uns to do in the heir of the Walpole fortunes, lass," he said, giving her a twisted grin. "Better luck next time, eh?"

She noticed the knife in the dust. "Did they try to use that on you?"

"One of several weapons which were brought into play," Walpole answered.

"I wonder," she said, "if they were really pickpockets."

"Yes, yes," the eavesdropping shopkeeper assured her. "Pickpockets and nothing more. Pickpockets, plain and simple."

"No doubt." Walpole rubbed his knobby hands together. "Well, gov, I was on me way to meet you at the safari offices after a morning constitutional stroll. Shall we journey there together?"

"Okay, the safari we're signed up for is due to take off in an hour." Gypsy placed his hand briefly on his friend's shoulder.

"Let's be up and going."

The Black girl behind the lucite desk smiled hopefully. "It's not real," she explained, tugging at the lapels of her leopardskin suit. "We wouldn't dream of killing a real

leopard, even if we knew where to find one. So if—"

"He ain't nervy about that, mum," Walpole told the manager of the Quatermain offices.

"Often people are." The girl stood—she was nearly six feet tall—and approached Gypsy. "Therefore, I always explain that—"

"No need to apologize, it's a beano of a suit." Walpole watched her walk across the tree-lined room. "Believe I saw a bloke on Fleet Street in a suit of similar cut."

The Black girl paused, fondling her vest. "It's called the London Businessman Style, as a matter of fact. I have a bowler hat to go with it, made of rhino skin—imitation rhino."

Gypsy, hands behind his back, was studying a large illuminated pleximap which covered an office wall. "I'm surprised to see," he said, pointing at the intricacy of colored light-lines on the trek map, "that there are two places called Ngumi. I hadn't noticed that when I was here before, and the charts I consulted—"

"You wouldn't want to visit either one, sir," the Black girl said, tucking her thumbs into her spotted vest pockets. "The one Ngumi is—"

"Why are there two, and why are they almost thirty miles apart?"

"If you'll note the parenthetical remarks . . . oh, they're dimmed out, hold it." She booted the lower extremity of the wall with her foot. "The boots aren't real alligator, by the way. There it is . . . See, the Ngumi over there is also known as Model Africa, and the Ngumi down that way is still only just plain Ngumi. Both rotten places, as I may have mentioned, and Quatermain wouldn't touch either with—"

"Which one is the real Ngumi?"

"Both, sir."

"How is that?" Gypsy asked.

"Something like ten years ago they had an urban renewal movement that got out of hand. Before the fighting was over roughly half of Ngumi had been relocated down there. Supposed to be better irrigation potential there."

"You mean they actually moved part of the city itself? Buildings and all?"

"Trees, buildings, subsoil. It was a real miracle of technology," said the girl in the leopard suit. "Seems like a waste, considering what rotten places both Ngumis are. I believe they had help from the United States, which still went in for—"

"Our safari route takes us closest to the first Ngumi," Gypsy observed. "The one better known now as Model Africa."

The girl put her hand on his arm. "I sincerely hope you don't bolt your trek and try to go to Ngumi. Either Ngumi. Because if you get murdered in your bed, rent asunder, cruelly mangled, or—"

"You've nothing to fear, mum," said Walpole. "The gov is merely curious about the bleeding fascinating history of Africa. I've been on treks and expeditions with him before and he trods the straight and narrow, he does."

Gypsy turned his back on the glowing map. "*Two* of them," he said quietly. "Hadn't expected that."

"Be a good sport."
"No, thanks."
"*I'm* wearing one."
"So I noticed."
"Gives me a tough-guy look, right? Worn at a cocky angle it exudes romance. Come on, don't be a jerk."

Gypsy once more shook his head. "I don't need one."

Lars Westchester was a large man, sun-cooked and bleached. He was holding a sun helmet out to Gypsy, a hat similar to the one he wore, at a cocky angle, on his pale-blonde head. "People go on a safari, they wear this kind of topper. Get it? It's part of what you call the mystique of the whole frigging mess." He wagged the proffered hat a few more times. "It'll look damned good on you. 'Specially if you wear it at a jaunty tilt. Come along, be a good sport. I like everybody on my safaris to look smart." He gestured at the others gathered in the compound behind the Quatermain, Inc. offices. "Mr. Fischoff is wearing his pith helmet, Mrs. Lambdin's got one on her dome, so has old Steffanson. Miss Tara's wearing one of the frigging things—not quite cocky enough, Miss Tara—and both Mr. and Mrs. Brinkerhoff are sporting sun helmets. Even your two chums got them."

Gypsy said, "Okay, I'll take one." He remembered he was trying to pass as a simple tourist.

"Good enough, pal," said Westchester, chuckling. "It'll keep the sun out, too. Hell of a lot better than that silly handkerchief you got on your coco at the moment."

Walpole poked his tongue into his cheek when Gypsy topped himself with the pith helmet. "Fetching," he observed. "Gives you a touch of the trad jungle romance." He was standing near the pole-fence of the compound, close to the five Black men who were playing the parts of bearers on the upcoming hundred-mile hike.

"Your young man is quite attractive," Mrs. Lambdin whispered to Annabelle. "Or is it the skinny one you're attached to?"

"We're all of us simply good friends," replied the girl. She had the feeling her own helmet was a size too large.

"It's delightful for you to be able to go on a safari

while still young," said the frail old woman.

"If you must go at all," said Annabelle.

"Ah, I've dreamed, child, of a safari since I was a wee nubbins of a girl." Mrs. Lambdin's eyes drifted almost shut. "Ever since I saw, back when the world was whole, a motion picture about a gentleman who was billed as the king of the jungle. He wore a very skimpy costume fashioned from animal hide and was very good at swinging through the trees. A marvelous actor by the name of Hunnker played the role and I even joined a Hunnker Fan Club. Of course when the world went blooey, it took fan clubs with it."

Annabelle asked, "Do you think you're going to be up to a long jaunt in the wilds?"

"I'm much sturdier than I look. Diet and exercise is what accounts for it," confided Mrs. Lambdin.

"Have you ever," Mr. Brinkerhoff ventured to ask Gypsy, "been on safari before?" He was a soft-spoken, redhaired man of forty-one. His pale skin was sprinkled with orange freckles. "I ask because I noticed you were somewhat scornful about the necessity of a sun helmet."

"Thought it looked silly," said Gypsy. "I'm sure, though, our guide—"

"Hey, would you mind referring to me as the White Hunter?" called Westchester from where he was inspecting the bearers' packs. "Adds to the frigging romance. Right?"

"White Hunter," said Gypsy with a grin.

"You don't look silly in that helmet," Mrs. Brinkerhoff, a pretty woman of thirty-seven, told him. "You look very handsome. I only wish Stephen here came across so . . . debonair."

"I look pretty good." Brinkerhoff adjusted the stiff brim of his sun hat. "That's surely a cocky angle, isn't it?"

"Cocky, possibly, but not quite debonair," his wife said. "Don't fret about it, Stephen, you simply don't have the right-shape skull to bring it off."

"What's wrong with my skull, Eve? You've never before comment—"

"Nothing, nothing, sweetheart. I love your skull. I love you—and *all* your bones."

"Isn't that how we met: you saw me across the room at the Democratic Commandos Box Social? It was, as I remember the event, the pleasing shape of my head which attracted you to me."

"Your skull is certainly distinctive, and different, Stephen," acknowledged Eve Brinkerhoff. "All I'm saying is that when you put a pith helmet on it, you don't come off quite as debonair as . . . what is your name?"

"They call me Gypsy."

"That's very distinctive. Isn't it, Stephen?"

"If you go for terse names." He removed his helmet, tapped at its apex with his forefinger. "That's your whole and entire name?"

Gypsy answered, "At the moment."

"Okay, folks," announced Westchester, "enough social gabbing. Now we move out." He raised both arms high. "You all signed the frigging release forms, but let me remind you that Quatermain, Inc. isn't responsible if you're attacked or eaten by wild animals . . . that includes real animals and robot simulacra. Also we ain't to blame should you fall into quicksand, catch the jungle rot, get cooked by hostile savages, or sold into bondage by slavers. We do, however, provide all meals and cater to all existing dietary laws. Line up and we'll get going on our trek."

"There wasn't anything about quicksand in the brochure, Eve."

"You missed it, Stephen, right next to the picture of

the cannibal banquet."

"We'll be walking for the next few hours," said Westchester as two of the bearers swung the wooden compound gates open, "through Quatermain, Inc.'s simulated jungle. In it you got the best plants, trees, wildlife, and so on from all over Africa. That's best and most popular, according to surveys carried on among folks pretty much like yourselves. This leg of the trip you'll get used to safariing. When we reach real, unimproved Africa, you'll be ready to cope with it. Okay? Let me remind you, by the way, to stick with our group all the time. No wandering off on your own. Especially when we pass near the country of Model Africa. You don't want to go in there."

"Danger and peril," sighed Mrs. Lambdin. "Exactly what I imagined. It's going to be marvelous."

"At the very least," agreed Annabelle.

FOURTEEN

Boom!
Baroom!
Boom!
"Too loud you think maybe?"
"A shade, yes."
Westchester nodded in agreement. He had dropped back along the single file of the trek to walk beside Annabelle for a moment.
Boom! Kaboom!
"When we get to the next rest station I'll call the head office and tell them to turn down the volume."
"Why are we having drums anyway?" asked Annabelle.
"What do you mean? You *got* to have native drums in the jungle." He jerked a sunburned thumb at the transplanted jungle they were marching through. Giant trees, ferns, palms, spiky bushes, flowering vines crowded all around the paved safari trail. Green was everywhere, a hundred shades of it. The afternoon sun was considerably screened by the foliage interlocked overhead.
Boom!
Kabloom!
Boom! Boom!
"Can we assume," Mr. Brinkerhoff said to his wife, "that these drums are not manned by those cannibals he was talking about?"
His wife glanced back over her slim shoulder at him. Pointing upward, she said, "Only part of the illusion, Stephen. The noise comes out of loudspeakers like that one dangling there."
"We really have no reason to believe the cannibals aren't capable of using radio."
"Relax, Stephen, and enjoy the safari."
Walpole was trudging at the rear of the line, with Gypsy ahead of him. "That old dame," he remarked in a low

voice, "that Mrs. Lambdin, seems to be holding up bloody well."

"And?"

"Been toying with the notion, gov—she ain't as old as she's got up to be."

Gypsy said, "She seems authentic enough to me."

"Could be I'm overly nervy," admitted the lanky young man. "The crux of the whole blinking problem is, I don't think them Scavengers are simply going to up and leave us alone. Leave *you* alone, I mean to say. They were damned determined to bag you, gov."

"From what you've told me," said Gypsy as he moved back to Walpole's side, "they still aren't sure of me, of exactly what I'm capable of doing." He hesitated, grinning. "But then, neither am I."

"Oh, to be sure, them blokes are wary of you," said his friend. "Don't forget, however, they made an all-out try to catch you when you came to wrest me from their perishing clutches."

"They *made* a try—I overcame it."

"You think that got the wind up for them? That they're going to leave you alone henceforth?"

"These Scavengers may want to do more digging into my background before they try another grab," said Gypsy.

Walpole sucked his cheek in and shrugged lopsidedly. "Even so, gov, that don't rule out the blinking possibility they've set spies to keep an eye on us."

"No, it doesn't."

"They got themselveves a darn good network for gathering info. I mean to say, they kept tabs on me, snatched me up when they wanted me. So it ain't exactly beyond the—"

"Good heavens! Help!" It was old Mrs. Lambdin, midway in the procession. She had halted and was gestur-

ing at the trees rising up by this section of trail.

"Knock it off, will you?" yelled the safari leader. "All part of the show."

Five ample gorillas were standing in the crisscross shadows.

"Blimey, not more apes," said Walpole. "I still ain't over that mechanical bunch we met up with on Gibraltar."

"They'll eat us," said Mr. Brinkerhoff.

"Gorillas are vegetarians," Mr. Fischoff informed him.

"*These* gorillas aren't meateaters *or* vegetarians," announced Westchester, removing his pith helmet and scratching at his short-cropped blonde hair. "They're nothing more than brilliantly crafted robots, placed here to entertain you."

"Entertain?" said Mrs. Lambdin. "What do they *do*? I hope it isn't singing."

"They entertain," Westchester explained, "by being gorillas."

"Wouldn't real gorillas be less expensive?" asked Brinkerhoff.

"We found real ones aren't as entertaining," the guide said. "Let's resume our trek."

"Never trust them gadgets," Walpole swallowed as they passed the watchful robots. "Rather have a true-life gorilla any day."

The party traveled another mile-and-a-half into the believable jungle before the crashing and thrashing was heard.

"That noise makes me uneasy," said Mrs. Lambdin.

"Nothing to worry about," Westchester assured her. "All part of the . . . oops." He pressed his lips shut, increasing his pace.

Mr. Brinkerhoff inquired, "What was that 'oops' for?"

"Just an 'oops,' " said the guide. "A nervous habit of mine—you should excuse it."

"Well, why are you nervous?"

Crackle!

Crash!

Kabang!

"I'm not exactly *nervous*."

"What exactly is the entertainment value of all that crash-bang stuff?" Mrs. Lambdin wanted to know. "Frankly, I wasn't all that taken with those stupid gorillas, and this is even dumber."

Halting, Westchester signaled them to do likewise. "Let me be honest. Okay? There's a possibility we've run into Grouchy."

"Grouchy?" said Mr. Fischoff as he fanned himself with his sun helmet. "What is Grouchy?"

Crack!

Bam!

Crackle!

"He's . . ." said Westchester, eyes on the darkening jungle to his right, "sort of a robot gorilla."

Old Mrs. Lambdin said, "You told us we didn't have to worry about them."

"Them, no. Him, yes."

"Wait now," said Mr. Fischoff. "I remember now—I heard rumors about this baby. He's a rogue, a robot who's gone absolutely goofy."

"He *is* less *docile* than the others," admitted Westchester.

"He's a *killer*," said Fischoff. "Runs wild, rips up animals, people, anything. Your staff hasn't been able to bag him."

"We have hundreds of smoothly functioning robots," said the guide. "But the one single one who—"

"Kill! Kill!" An enormous redhaired gorilla came

leaping out of the jungle and onto the path some twenty yards ahead of them. "Kill! Kill all!"

"Why, he can talk!" noticed Mrs. Brinkerhoff.

"He wasn't supposed to." Westchester, drawing a stungun, was very slowly approaching the crazed mechanism.

"How come he's a redhead?" asked redhaired Brinkerhoff. "Is that somebody's idea of a joke?"

"He did it himself," said Fischoff. "I remember reading about him, made the dye from roots and berries. He's one very independent robot."

"He'll murder us all," said Mrs. Lambdin.

"Perhaps, Stephen, you ought to lend a hand," suggested Mrs. Brinkerhoff to her husband.

Saying nothing, Gypsy ran along the trail. He soon passed the hesitant Westchester.

"Kill! Kill 'em all!" The gorilla snarled, pounding its hairy chest.

"Back into the jungle!" Gypsy, hands on hips, had halted a few feet from the wild robot.

"You first!" Tucking its shaggy head into its shaggy shoulders, the renegade robot came charging at him.

Gypsy dodged and thrust out a foot.

The gorilla tripped and hit the asphalt trail with a great thumping thud. "Dirty trick," it muttered.

Gypsy didn't wait for him to get up. He grabbed the kneeling robot by its shoulders. "Into the jungle, as I advised." With no effort Gypsy lifted up the giant mechanism, raised it completely over his head, and threw it clear.

Grouchy sailed, like an enormous hairy pinwheel, for about ten feet before hitting branches and vines. His flight diminished from that point, making increasing noise. He landed some distance from the trail, festooned with shreds of vine, twists of branches, ripped flower

petals. He did not rise.

Thirty seconds of silence followed.

Then Westchester said, "Okay, let's move on. Nothing to see here." He trotted up to Gypsy, clapped him on the shoulder. "Good job, better than I could have done. Thanks."

"Welcome," said Gypsy.

FIFTEEN

Out here everything had long since fallen down. The Big Quake had done that, sent all the buildings on the hillside along this stretch of beach tumbling down, only to be broken up on the rocky shore. Restaurants, a hotel, all were now mounds of rusted metal, splintered wood, broken glass. Weathered now, worm-eaten, speckled with gull droppings, blotched with fungus.

Jackita Teal ignored the ruins, walking stiffly along the edge of the Pacific. She watched the early morning ocean, the fog-blurred Farallon Islands. "We learn by such experiences, Pres," she was saying.

Following her, panting, the heavyset Preston Bookings said, "I don't think the whole control committee agrees."

"Perhaps not—but enough *do*."

A single gull came skimming low along the water.

The gaunt woman stopped to look at it. The breeze coming in from the horizon fluttered her grey cloak. "We learned that we must approach Gypsy very cautiously."

"We already knew that," said Bookings, sucking in a breath. "The fellow can't be taken over by the Scavengers until we know everything about him. Consider, reflect on, the damage he did to our facility at São Tiago. The cost of—"

"The cost isn't important, not when compared to our final objective," she said. "Gypsy can help there. I'm certain, after having studied Dr. Hawksworth's journals . . . something, by the way, you ought to do."

"I'm not an enormous fan of vain women," he said, stopping still to wipe the sweat from his face. "I skimmed the lady's journals, getting all the information I need. I see no necessity of savoring every line."

"You're a throwback, Pres, to the last century at *least*."

Bookings lowered himself onto a driftwood log, dabbing at his forehead and cheeks. "You've got to let Gypsy continue this quest of his," he told the lean woman. "Let him unearth the remaining information *for* us. When he puts all the pieces together, then we can move to assimilate him."

Jackita nodded. "Yes, I'm allowing him to complete the African phase of Dr. Hawksworth's game."

"Then we needn't take any further—"

"Yes, I want to get rid of his friends."

"Gypsy is the one to worry about. He's the lad who outwitted our weapons and gimmicks on São Tiago, so why—"

"They're an encumbrance. He continually allows himself to be sidetracked by those two. When Annabelle and Walpole are out, then Gypsy will concentrate on the quest."

"Yes, but I really don't see the need to—"

"They're to be taken from him, then killed."

"Not a wise move at all. It will only make him angry. He'll certainly try to revenge himself—"

"Nevertheless, I've already set the process in motion," she cut in. "His friends will be taken from this ridiculous safari he's using as an excuse to get to Ngumi. They'll be executed, and then Gypsy will get on with his real business."

"I tell you, it . . . what's *that*?"

The gaunt woman spun in time to see a large dark bird rise up from the ruins of an ancient souvenir shop. "The vulture!" she cried. "The damned *vulture*!" Her long fingers had drawn a blaster pistol from beneath her cloak.

Jackita fired twice up into the morning sky. But the vulture was no longer there.

They caught him.

He couldn't run anymore; his legs ached, and each breath that he sucked in rasped through him. Gypsy staggered, tried to push them away, then fell.

They caught him. They were all over him, smashing, punching, clawing, slashing. The various pains merged into one enormous one, exploding inside Gypsy, ripping . . .

Wait. His name hadn't been Gypsy then. No. Fifty years ago he was called . . .

Nothing.

He couldn't remember.

And another dream came. Shadows, everyone in heavy coats, breath coming out in misty swirls. Gathered around him.

". . . do perfectly."

"She won't be able to get away with it."

"Why not?"

"Not with *him*. After what he's done."

"She can arrange things. This is too good an opportunity to pass."

"He's fallen into our hands. We'll make use of him."

"Never get away with it."

Sunlight. Thousands of leaves overhead, autumn colors. The old man—only he wasn't old—looking down at him.

"Coming along fine. There's no need to worry."

A different sun. The old man was old now. ". . . managed to save you," he was saying. "And that creature as well, though I have, Gypsy, mixed feelings about it. Still you may need, as originally planned, some sort of guide after . . ."

"Touch of the sun, gov?"

Gypsy blinked. He was standing in a hot morning street, and a few yards ahead of him began a row of shops

built of stucco and mosaic tile. A lightstrip sign mounted on bamboo posts announced it as *Maziko Village Souvenir Mall*. "Mind was wandering," he said.

"Might be a better occupation than touring this perishing sucker trap yonder."

"Mrs. Brinkerhoff assures me it's charming," put in Annabelle.

The rest of the safari, trailing Westchester, was moving in among the settlement of shops.

"Was more of the good old days rambling through your mind?" Walpole asked as they went walking after the rest of the trek party.

Gypsy nodded. "I'm seeing more and more pieces of the damned jigsaw, but I still can't fit them together in any kind of—"

"Rugs, sahib? Rugs, mem? Near-authentic treasures from ancient African lands!" A rug merchant in a suit made of fuzzy carpet samples was beckoning to them.

"Nomads got no perishing use for rugs, mate," Walpole explained in passing.

Gypsy glanced across the street, noticing something flash in a shop window. "Think I'll explore over there a minute." He trotted off for the jeweler's shop alone.

What he'd seen was a gemstone that appeared exactly like an eye of his persistent vulture. It rested on a swatch of frayed velvet, glowing in the sunlight. There were heavy metal armbands, bone necklaces, beads and bracelets tumbled and spilled in the display window, but only the eyestone glowed in that particular way.

The narrow shop was empty of customers. Slouched behind the counter was a pale, seedy man in a beaded suit. "Don't be afraid of a little illness, sir. Come right in. Plenty of bargains to be had in old Nezakonit's Bazaar. I am none other than Nezakonit himself."

"You have a—"

"Don't let my red blotches spook you. It's only the last traces of a mild little plague." Nezakonit poked at various fiery red patches on his puffy face. "When you get to be my age, you catch every plague that comes along. Something nice in a timepiece, perhaps?"

"In your window is a—"

"Ah, the window," sighed the shopkeeper. "That presents a problem, young stranger, since I'm also recuperating from a bout of paralysis. Nothing catching. No need to fear. It simply means I can't fetch merchandise out of the display window without experiencing severe—"

"I know what I want." Gypsy strode to the sliding panel which opened onto the display.

"Old Nezakonit will have to trust you, young sir. Assume you mean him no ill and will not snatch priceless African curiosities from—"

"Can you tell me where you got this?" Gypsy had removed the jewel-eye off its cloth and was holding it at arm's length.

"Resembles an eye, doesn't it? In fact, I wish *I* had a glass eye half so fine. Mine, as you've no doubt noticed, is much inferior." With considerable effort the old man raised a hand and tapped his thumb against his left eye. "I was visited with some foul disease two winters since which caused—"

"This stone." Gypsy held it close to the shopman's good eye. "I want to know where it came from."

"Every jewel, every precious artifact in the shop of old Nezakonit has a fascinating story to tell. Yet these timid tourists shun me merely because I suffer from a few . . . Ag! Ag! Hak! Hak!" He commenced coughing violently.

Gypsy slapped him across the back. "Take it easy."

"Ag! Ag! Haka-hak! Hak!" The shopkeeper left off coughing and slumped further into his wicker chair. "Not fatal lung disease at all, young sir, but only a mild allergic reaction. Let me offer now to your eager ears the astounding tale of how . . . Ag! Ag! Haka! Nothing to worry about, a trivial spasm. This stone was brought to me by a young Black fellow who was fleeing for his life."

"Fleeing from where?"

"Ag! Ag! Hackyhacky! Don't worry, young gentleman, old Nezakonit isn't spewing fatal germs upon you. The fellow who brought this rare treasure had recently fled from Ngumi and—"

"*Which* Ngumi?"

"It was . . . Yow! Wow! Yow!" Nezakonit managed to make his gnarled right hand slap at the side of his head. "Nothing you can catch, young sir—simply a moderately horrible attack of the migraine. What was I saying? Ah, yes . . . Yow! Wow! Owie! *Which* Ngumi? Yes, it was the one they now refer to as Model Africa—a fearful place, from what I hear. My impression is this fellow found this rare gem in a place he wasn't supposed to be. I never delve too deeply into such matters."

The gem, Gypsy decided, almost certainly came from a creature like the vulture, which meant Model Africa was likely to be the Ngumi he wanted. Gypsy said, "How much do you . . ." but didn't complete the sentence. He frowned, listening.

"Having a sudden spasm, young gentleman?"

"I thought I heard someone calling me," answered Gypsy. "Must have been mistaken. I'd like to buy this. What's the price?"

"A treasure such as this . . . Yow! Wow! . . . Ag! Ag! Hacky-hack! . . . Well, considering the delicate condition I'm in, old Nezakonit won't argue. A hundred dollars."

"Fifty," countered Gypsy.

"Ag! Ag! Hacky!"

"Fifty."

"Sold," said the old shopkeeper.

"No need to wrap it." Gypsy placed the agreed-on sum on the countertop and dropped the eye into a pocket.

"You took advantage of me, young sir, but no matter. Fifty dollars in the till is better than a touch of the plague, as my people say."

"A wise insight." Gypsy left the sick man's place of business.

He didn't see either Walpole or Annabelle outside. Gypsy started up one side of the souvenir mall, checking into each shop with no success. When he passed the alley between an imitation animal skin boutique and a restaurant advertising cannibal-style cooking, a voice in the shadows called out to him. "Trouble's brewing, Gypso."

The vulture was perched in there, claws on the chest of the flat-out Lars Westchester. The guide was snoring in a jerky way, his pith helmet lying in the dirt near his head.

"What happened to him?" Gypsy crouched beside the sprawled man.

"Stunguns. He'll snap out of it in a couple hours. Meantime you better go right to this Ngumi—whichever one you pick—and forget about Walpole and the girl. I don't—"

"What are you babbling about? Where are they?"

"You're not paying attention, kid. I'm breaking my neck telling you not to search for them and you—"

"You *know*, don't you?"

"While you were frequenting the quaint shops your chums were stungunned and carted off by two members of your own safari. Larso here noticed it and attempted to keep them from dumping your buddies into a handy skyvan but—"

"Who took Annabelle and Walpole?"

"That nice Brinkerhoff couple," replied the vulture.

"Who would have guessed such mild and likable folks worked for the Scavengers? My land, a body just can't—"

"So the Scavengers are behind the grab?"

"Righto, Gyp. Once again the long arm of the sinister—"

"Where did they take my friends?"

"Hey, it's no concern of yours. Yours is but to get to the real and authentic Ngumi. Besides which, old pal, Model Africa is reputed to be a nice place to avoid. If that is where the likable Brinkerhoffs are taking your friends."

Gypsy grinned at the hunched bird. "You know damn well I'm going to trail them there," he said. "You're goading me, you want to make sure I do." He pointed at the vulture. "I know that Model Africa was once part of Ngumi, too. So don't try to con me into maybe looking in the wrong place. I'll check out both Ngumis—after I get Walpole and Annabelle back from those damned Scavengers."

"Trust me, Gyps," said the bird. "The stuff you seek is at the other Ngumi. Model Africa is only a waste of time for you."

"What about *this*?" Gypsy showed him the gem-eye he'd just purchased.

"Saw something like that once. It was the prize in a carton of candied popcorn." The giant wings fluttered. The vulture all at once vanished, the air crackling as it went.

SEVENTEEN

The tower stood in isolation. A pale blue in color, it rose out of the yellow plain to a height of several hundred feet. Gypsy frowned as he approached it through the early morning. He knew he was nearing Model Africa and decided to climb the lonely tower. From its top he'd be able to see the place that used to be called Ngumi.

Several dusky-brown birds fluttered up out of the high grass, frightened by his coming.

In the weedy courtyard of the cylindrical tower he noticed a tilted sign: *A Magnificent New Building Will Soon Appear On This Site! Another Model Africa Marvel!* The sign and its post were rich with encrusted bird droppings.

Gypsy made his way to the entryway. The metal door hung half-open. "Familiar," he murmured. "Something familiar about this place." A circular neometal staircase corkscrewed up inside the building, culminating in a glass-floored observation room. "Did that damned bird lie to me? Is this part of the facility?"

He took the upward steps two or three at a time, boots clanging on the rungs.

The warm morning air rushed at him when he reached the top of the blue tower. The neoglass walls had long ago been broken away up here.

To his left he saw a white glow which was Model Africa. Gypsy crossed the seethrough floor to—

Something over in the tumble of broken furniture on his right. Something hunched and watching.

"If this isn't the right place, what are *you* doing here?"

The vulture did not reply.

Gypsy came closer. "You're supposed to . . ." He realized this was not the same creature. Its feathers were dusty and it had only one eye. On an impulse, Gypsy took the gem out of his pocket and thrust it into the empty socket.

The bird's beak snapped open and shut; its wings unfurled once and then closed.

They must have built more than one of these damned things. If there was one to watch over him, maybe this one was designed to guard the secrets which must be hidden hereabouts. "What do you know about—"

Before Gypsy could complete the question the great bird flew straight at him.

He stumbled back.

The vulture's claws raked at his face and chest, forcing him further back. "Trespass!" it shrieked. "Trespass!"

Gypsy was about to grab at the winged creature's neck when he found himself stepping on air. He'd gone off the glass floor and was falling toward the faraway ground.

The vulture came swooping after him.

A voice—perhaps it was his own—said, "Force. Cushion with force."

Gypsy remembered something else. Twisting in the air, he pointed his hands at the uprushing ground. Beams of throbbing silver light came pouring from his fingertips. He ceased falling. He was holding himself in midair with some sort of force beams which he could generate.

With the vulture clawing at his back, Gypsy gently lowered himself to the grassy plain.

The bird flapped away, then dived at his head.

He caught it by the throat. The beak slashed his cheek. With one powerful twist he broke its neck and the bird ceased.

Dropping it to the ground, Gypsy crouched beside it. He took out a small knife to poke and prod at the thing.

Soon he discovered it was an intricately constructed mechanism and not a real bird at all. In a small copper compartment in the vulture's inner workings he found a metal rod about three inches long. It was a clouded grey and seemed not to be a part of the actual mechanism. He took it in his hand. "I think I'm supposed to use this," he said to himself, striving to remember, ". . . later."

"Knocked off the black sheep, huh?"

He glanced up to see his old familiar vulture circling downward. "How many of you are there?"

"We're a vanishing breed." The bird landed a safe distance from him. "Vanishing very rapidly."

"Are *you* like that inside?" Rising, Gypsy poked the gutted robot bird with his foot.

"I never answer intimate questions about my body, Gyp," replied the vulture. "Why are you dallying here when—"

"You told me the archives were elsewhere."

"And truth it was I spoke, laddy buck."

"Then why did I find this thing here and not at the other—"

"Part of the old facility is here in this half of Ngumi; the rest of it, underground parts and all, is at the other locale. The info you want, chum, is—"

"So you say."

"Hold your horses. You ought to know by now I never lie to you. Bend the truth, in the interest of good clean sport, but never fib."

Gypsy held out the rod between thumb and forefinger. "I have a hunch this is some sort of key."

"Might be, Gyp. I don't think a youth of your intelligence has to waste time rounding up keys, but suit yourself. Right now, though, time's a-wasting in the matter of your missing chums."

"Do you know exactly where they are?"

"Bon voyage, Gyp." The vulture climbed into the air, rising higher and higher away from Gypsy.

The whiteness of it dazzled. Standing on the wide main street of the capital city of Model Africa, Gypsy shaded his eyes with his right hand. The midday sun blazed, the spotless white buildings glowed. The streets and sidewalks, made of tough opaque plastic, were bright and free of dirt.

A Japanese tourist came out of a sundries shop unwrapping a packet of breath candy. Absently he dropped the outer wrapper to the pavement.

Crackle! Zizzle!

A stunbeam, mounted on a near lamppost, flashed once and hit the man square in the chest. He froze where he stood, hand halfway to his mouth.

Bong! Bom! Bong!

An alarm bell, planted under the paving, commenced sounding. Less than a minute later a white skycar landed a few feet from the stunned Japanese. A Black lawman and a White lawman, clad in yellow uniforms, hopped from the ship. They approached the man, taking hold of his arms.

"It's forbidden to litter, you see," the Black policeman said to Gypsy, smiling.

"I'll make a note."

"You can't have," the other cop explained while they carried the litterer to their craft, "any kind of model country if people infringe."

"Nobody wants a nation of scofflaws," his partner said.

The frozen tourist was heaved into a rear compartment, and its doors were slammed. The cops got back in, and the very clean skycar climbed away.

"Didn't even pick up the wrapper." The Black shopkeeper hurried out of the sundries store and stooped to scoop it up. "Not that I'm complaining. Oh, no, far from it."

Gypsy asked, "Not a good idea to complain?"

"This is a model state," the man said, his voice a little unsteady. "What could anyone complain about?"

"Suppose somebody does?"

"Then they become political prisoners." He headed for his doorway. "Interest you in any sundries?"

"Have all I need, thanks." Gypsy walked on through the bright, clean streets.

There were not many tourists in the capital. Quite a few of the shop proprietors hailed him as he went by. Gypsy was searching for one particular building. He'd seen it, quite clearly, in his mind while crossing the border of Model Africa. While filling out the entrance forms, loyalty oaths, and good-behavior agreements, Gypsy had a sudden vision. He knew he would find news of Walpole and Annabelle at the place he was seeing. These premonitions he had, as yet, no control over. But he knew they were valid. Knew he . . .

"There it is." Gypsy slowed. Directly across the street, next to the fortlike building which housed the Model Africa Postal Service, stood a four-story pale yellow building. It was built of blocks of neoplaz and tinted sheets of plex. *Cobb's Auberge* proclaimed a sign hanging from a second-floor balcony of the inn.

As Gypsy crossed the spotless road, noise erupted from the postal service ground floor. A long, thin Black man in a two-piece daysuit came running out.

"Forget it," the running man called over his shoulder. "I'll used it smashed." He had a battered package held against his side with his sharp elbow.

A White man in a one-piece blue uniform ran out on the steps. "You can't malign the Model Africa Postal Service and expect to—"

"My quick temper got the best of me for a moment," the man called, still running. "What difference does it make if somebody stepped on my ant farm?"

Zizzle!

The postal clerk had used a stungun on the dissatisfied customer.

Gypsy skirted the frozen man and cut across the street to the inn.

An immense portrait of a Black man with an eyepatch was unfurled on the lobby floor.

"Pick it up, do something!" A chunky man was doing a nervous dance at the edge of the fallen poster.

"Well, sir, it's heavy. We've got to figure out just how to do it." Two Black men in candy-stripe robes were on the opposite edge of the picture, which covered nearly all of the tiled floor.

"Hurry, hurry! If they don't get us for sacrilege to the president's picture, they'll nab us for littering. Ah, good day, sir. A room?"

"Picture fall down?"

"Yes, it belongs on yonder wall there." The chunky man indicated the wall. "If Sahara Slim were to learn—"

"*That's* Sahara Slim, the president of Model Africa?" Gypsy indicated the portrait with his foot.

"Don't step on his face," warned the anxious clerk. "That's a criminal offense."

"Move back a little," Gypsy advised the two porters. He concentrated on the huge poster and, in under fifteen seconds, it flapped up off the floor and returned to the wall. The eyelets at its upper edge clicked over the wall hooks.

"That was certainly an impressive trick, sir." The clerk scurried behind his desk. "How exactly did you accomplish it?"

"Has to do with leverage," said Gypsy as he approached the desk.

"I never quite understood that particular subject in

school. A room?"

"Possibly," replied Gypsy. "I think some friends of mine are registered here. A Mr. and Mrs. Brinkerhoff?"

The clerk shut his eyes. "Brinkerhoff, Brinkerhoff, Brinkerhoff. No, not here. I have a mind like a government computer—though less efficient, obviously."

"Redhaired man, with freckles, dark-haired woman, fairly attractive." Gypsy leaned an elbow on the sign-in counter. "Arrived early this morning."

"You must be thinking of Dr. and Mrs. Frazer," said the chunky clerk. "What gave you the notion their name was Dinglehoffer? No, it's Frazer. A brilliant man is Dr. Frazer, for an outlander. He and his charming wife are frequent visitors to our country."

"What room?"

"The same as usual, the President Sahara Slim Suite, 406-407." The clerk was studying Gypsy's face. "Are you absolutely certain you're a friend of theirs? I'd hate to—"

"You noticed what happened to the poster," said Gypsy. "You wouldn't want to end up hanging on the other wall."

"You're absolutely correct there, sir."

"Also you don't want to let Dr. and Mrs. Frazer know I'm going to drop in at their suite."

"Once again you're absolutely right," said the clerk in a dim voice.

Neither of them said anything when Gypsy suddenly appeared in the parlor of their suite.

Eve Frazer, wearing only a short plyorobe, and Stephen Frazer, still in his safari outfit, had been sitting on a rattan lounge with a cocktail shaker and two glasses on the rattan coffee table in front of them.

The table tipped over; the frosted cocktail shaker executed a somersault and spewed cracked ice and liquor. Before anything had hit the floor Frazer was on his feet with a stungun in his hand.

Gypsy nodded at the weapon; it leaped from the freckled man's grasp. "Where are—"

He hadn't anticipated the knife at all.

She had it concealed—he never did figure out where—on her body. She threw it while he was using his telekinetic powers on her husband's gun.

The blade sliced at his cheek as it flew by. Gypsy flinched and took an involuntary step backward.

The woman jumped. She got hold of his repaired arm and twisted it up behind his back. "Get the stungun," she ordered Frazer.

Gypsy dropped to his knees, rocked forward, and sent Eve spinning over his shoulders.

Her plyorobe went crackling off her body; she landed naked on the straw matting. "Stun him, Steve, stun the bastard!"

"Okay, Gypsy, don't—" Before the redhaired man could use the stungun he'd snatched up, Gypsy caused the weapon and the doctor to go slamming into the far wall. A tri-op picture of zebras fell to the floor.

Eve sprinted, ignoring her slumped husband, and caught hold of the stungun.

"Don't!" cautioned Gypsy. He was at her side before she could swing it in his direction. With a single down-chop of his hand he knocked the stungun away.

"Bastard!" she repeated.

"Where are Annabelle and Walpole?"

"Dead," she told him.

He rattled when he walked. Rattled, creaked, hissed, ratcheted. A huge man, seven feet high, silky black, wearing an eyepatch. Dressed in a one-piece yellow commandosuit. He was Sahara Slim, perpetual president of Model Africa, and he came striding along the long grey corridor heading for the rectangle of sunlight at its end. Rattling, creaking, hissing, ratcheting.

"Mr. President!"

"Mr. President!"

"Mr. President!"

The corridor guards saulted as he passed them. One Black guard, one White guard, alternating all along the grey passageway.

"Mr. President!"

"Mr. President!"

"Mr. President!"

You could hear the screaming now. The closer Sahara Slim got to the daylight, the louder the cries of pain became.

The president of Model Africa stepped out onto the testing ground. Head bobbing and creaking, he counted for a moment. "Wasteful, Jim."

He was a parody of a Black man, this bobbing character. He was out of place, a refugee from the stereotype-laden movies of the twentieth century. He was obviously patterned after the urban American pimp more than anything else. Yet here he was in Africa, and the sounds coming from his body were as unreal as the fact that he was running the affairs of a small country. He was a joke—and in a saner part of the continent he would be outside the palace walls, not behind them.

A fat blonde man in the yellow uniform of the MA Militia huffed over to him and saluted. "Beg pardon, Mr. President?"

"I was saying wasteful, Colonel. You know what I

mean, Jim? Look at how many you done used up today and it ain't hardly afternoon, you know."

After frowning up at the Black president, the fat colonel turned and counted. "Only twenty-five, that's not—"

"Twenty-six, Jim. That's wasteful," said Sahara Slim. He indicated the Militiamen scattered across the wide yellow field. "I ain't going to give you jokers fifty political prisoners a day to practice with if you can't not use 'em more sparing. You already got twenty-six corpses stacked up over there. You going to use the whole batch up before the afternoon break. *Then* what?"

"Well, there's always the paper work that—"

"Don't give me no jive about paper work," said Sahara Slim. "You supposed to be turning these dudes into killers."

"Difficult task, sir, if you're going to complain about every darn political prisoner we kill," said the blonde colonel. "Now what about the pair the Scavengers donated? You won't let us use them until—"

"Told you about it already, Jim. Don't go jumping bad. I wants to talk with them two before you kill 'em," said the president. "See, if you get what I mean, I like to find out what's shaking. Before you jokers practice on these folks, I jaw with 'em a little. Find out something, maybe. About them, about the Scavengers."

"They look quite trivial to me, hard to believe they pose any real threat to the Scavengers."

"Where'd you stick 'em?"

"Over in Cage 3."

Ratcheting and creaking, Sahara Slim walked across the sunlit ground to the cage in question. "How you doing? I'm the president."

"Good," said Walpole, stepping closer to the thick iron bars, "because I got a complaint to make and it might as well start at the top."

"Hold on, Jim. I come to ask you folks some—"

"We have a few things to ask *you* first," said Annabelle. "Such as why we're being detained here. Why—"

"You're political prisoners," explained Sahara Slim.

"Says who?" asked Walpole. "We get stunned by that perishing Brinkerhoff couple and turned over to some of your twits and we end up in a cage with ringside seats to some kind of blooming massacre. If this all don't violate a bloke's civil rights, I don't know what does."

The president laughed and rattled. "Everybody got lots of civil rights in Model Africa," he said. "That's part of my platform."

"How come *we* don't, mate?"

"Everybody 'cept political prisoners," the president amplified. "As for what's going on around you, Jim, it ain't no massacre. This is merely a militia exercise, to test out new methods of crowd control and what-all."

"That's a good way to control them," said the girl. "Kill them dead, stack them up."

Sahara Slim said, "Yeah, it's been working real good for us. See, in order . . . holy mackerel!"

"It's the gov."

Gypsy had materialized beside the cage. "I'm *not* too late," he said.

"That's okay, that's okay. Get back to your spots." The president was waving off the guards who had noticed the advent of Gypsy and had come trotting over. "Can you explain me how you do that, Jim, that popping-out-of-nothing business?"

"I came," Gypsy announced, "to collect my friends."

"You don't want to mess with political prisoners. You mess 'round with political prisoners, that makes *you* a political prisoner."

Gypsy walked closer to the big man. "You're the presi-

dent, huh?"

"Sure am, Jim. And I bet I can whip your ass."

"That a challenge?"

"Heck, yes," Sahara Slim told him. "If I can't, which don't hardly seem likely, then you can take these folks off with you. That's fair, ain't it?" He glanced at the fat blonde colonel and winked.

"Fair, oh, yes, fair," agreed the colonel, chuckling.

When the president reached up to scratch his cheek, his arm made a rasping, grinding noise. "Maybe, Jim, I ought to warn you," he said through a broad smile. "I ain't exactly one hundred percent human. I'm one of them cyborgs, been rebuilt considerable. You know, it don't matter how good a security force you got, every now and then one of these assassin jokers is going to score. Thanks to the advanced scientific knowledge which abounds in Model Africa I been fixed up each time. I got to tell you I'm about ten times as good as I was, and even when I was just good I could of beat your butt into the ground."

"We'll see," said Gypsy.

"You going to, that's right."

"That's right, that's right," echoed several of the uniformed quards.

"Let's cease the militia practice for a while," ordered the president.

All the activity in the stone-walled field ceased. The Militiamen and the surviving political prisoners all watched the president and Gypsy.

"Where I really shines is in free-for-all fighting," Sahara Slim confided. "That style okay by you?"

"Fine," replied Gypsy. "One other thing. If I win, you let all the remaining prisoners go."

"*All*, Jim?"

"The people here, the ones in the pens under this

place—*all*."

Sahara Slim watched him for several seconds, then laughed. "Okay. If you win, you got it. That's *if.*"

"That's *if*, that's *if*," said the guards and the Militiamen.

"Can the colonel here see to that?"

"In case I ain't in any shape to?" Sahara Slim bent over to laugh and whap at his knee. The knee clanged when he smacked it. "Sure, Jim, he can."

Gypsy pointed at the man. "I'll expect you to carry out the president's promise. The prisoners, every one of them, are to be released and given safe conduct out of Model Africa."

The blonde colonel chuckled. "But of course."

"That's enough promising." Sahara Slim suddenly lowered his head, came charging at Gypsy, and butted him in the stomach.

The force of the blow slapped Gypsy back against the bars of the cage that held his friends.

"Watch him, gov," warned Walpole. "The cove don't fight fair."

"Wasn't expecting he would." Gypsy sidestepped the next charge, spun, and caught Sahara Slim by the left arm, twisting and pulling it.

This brought the president stretched up straight with his left arm behind his back. "Not bad, Jim." He gave out a rasping, clicking, ripping sound and jumped clear of Gypsy.

Gypsy was still holding the Black man's arm and the sleeve which encased it.

"Told you I was built a little special." Hunched, single arm dangling, Sahara Slim circled his opponent.

When he made his next growling lunge Gypsy used the left arm as a bat, delivering a sturdy clout to Sahara Slim's head.

"That's the bloody ballgame," observed Walpole. "He's finished."

The president's head had come clean off his neck. It was rolling in the dust.

Gypsy turned away from the swaying body of Sahara Slim.

"Watch out!" cried Annabelle.

The headless body was stalking Gypsy. The right fist dealt a sharp, stunning blow to the back of Gypsy's neck that knocked him forward and down.

"It ain't over yet, Jim. It's only just getting good."

On his hands and knees, vision fuzzy, Gypsy saw the president walk over and pick up his head with his remaining arm. He clicked it back into place.

"Did I mention," the Black man inquired, "I was only about just one step from being a robot? Yeah, Jim, you can take me apart and it don't worry me none. 'Cause I can put myself back together again. Even wear me a special breakaway suit."

As Gypsy attempted to rise, Sahara Slim ran straight at him to boot him hard in the chin.

Teeth clicking, Gypsy was driven to his knees, pain exploding inside his skull. He tried to dodge the next kick, but it took him in the ribs.

"Foul!" cried Walpole from his cage.

On all fours, Gypsy scurried for safety, retreating from the Black man.

"Got him running now," boasted the president. "Got him . . . hey!"

His right arm had vanished. It had pulled free of his body, hovered a few inches from his torso, and then faded into nothingness.

Armless, Sahara Slim moved to where his left arm had fallen. He was about to kick at it when that limb, too, popped away.

"The gov's teleporting his ruddy parts away." Walpole nudged Annabelle.

"So I guessed," she said.

"Can still stomp you with my . . . wow!" His right leg was tugged free of his body. It rose, bright-booted, up into the air.

Before the leg had vanished high above them, the remaining leg was gone as well.

The president's heavy torso thumped to the ground. It rocked and fell over on its backside. "This ain't fair," he complained.

Gypsy crossed and stood over him. "We never said anything about *fair*. Do you concede?"

"I ain't finished yet, Jim."

"If you quit now," Gypsy said down to what was left of the president, "you'll get yourself back once everyone is clear of Model Africa. But if I send your head where your arms and legs went . . ."

"I was expecting a contest of strength, Jim, not some damned mumbo jumbo."

"You concede or not?" Gypsy squatted beside him, eyeing his head.

"Okay, okay. You win."

Straightening, Gypsy noticed the blonde Militia colonel. "You can start releasing the prisoners. My friends here first."

"Sir?" The plump colonel shuffled over, staring down at the remains of Sahara Slim.

"Yeah, yeah. A deal's a deal," said the president. "He whupped me, so keep the promise. I want my parts back."

"Would you like me to cover you with a tarp, sir, until—"

"Turn them prisoners free. Right *now*, you hear?"

The cloudy sky was a smudged blue; the high yellow grass crackled as they trudged across the late afternoon plain.

"Don't like to be a perishing wet blanket, gov," said Walpole, poking a finger skyward, "but ain't that your bloody vulture a-circling over there."

A large dark bird was arcing through the air above a stand of flat-topped trees about a quarter-mile ahead of them.

"It might be," said Gypsy, glancing in that direction.

"He wouldn't," suggested Annabelle, "keep such a distance between us. Not Gypsy's vulture—he'd be right close, heckling."

"Coo," said Walpole, "then maybe that's a real blooming vulture."

"A real scavenger," said the girl.

Walpole broke his stride and executed a few hops. "That there critter might be getting ready to light on some dead bloke. That's what vultures do, ain't it?"

"More likely a dead animal," said Gypsy. "These plains between Model Africa and Ngumi aren't supposed to be populated anymore."

Walpole continued to move forward somewhat jerkily. "I wouldn't want to witness no giraffe or zebra or whatever being brunched on by some bloody bird."

"Squeamish," said Annabelle. "Wouldn't have suspected that from someone with your background."

"Ain't nothing wrong with me background, I'll have you know. My mum was quite a high-class . . . Say! It's a man!" He went running ahead through the dry, clattering grass.

Gypsy followed. "Hold it," he shouted. "Don't go barging into anything."

"Get away, shoo! Go on, you ninny! Animal Dan's a long way from dead." Sprawled against the trunk of one of the thorn trees was a very old man. He wore a pair of frayed khaki shorts, boots, and a peaked cap. His white beard spilled down across his tan leathery chest. Shaking a weathered fist at the circling bird, he added, "Go on about your business. When Animal Dan does cash in his chips, you'll get an invitation."

"You okay, old chap?" Walpole was cautiously approaching Animal Dan.

"Sure I am, you ninny. And where do you get off calling me old? Is ninety-six *your* idea of old?"

"Up until now, yes," admitted Walpole as he took three steps closer. "You injured?"

"You're worse than that feebleminded vulture," said Animal Dan. "A man can't take a little walk and pause to catch his breath without somebody calling the funeral parlor and making a reservation. Who are you and why are you trespassing?"

"Trespassing?" Annabelle joined them.

"Oh, hellfire and thunderation," sighed Animal Dan, "you went and brought a female into Animal Dan's Domain. Bad luck. Who knows better than me? I had the lack of sense to import not one but two females in here over the last fifty years. Each brought me enough ill luck to . . . go away, you idiot bird!" He gave the still-hovering vulture the finger while struggling to his feet.

Gypsy asked, "You've lived hereabouts for fifty years?"

The old man was swaying from left to right, but he managed to get himself up. "You look like you might have a lick of sense," Animal Dan told Gypsy. "I can't imagine you haven't heard of me: Animal Dan."

"Afraid not. My name is Gypsy and—"

"Never heard of Animal Dan? Never heard of Animal Dan's Domain? Where've you been?"

"That's what I'm here to find out."

"You never saw the movies?"

"Are you an oldtime actor?" asked Annabelle.

"Actor? Oh, what a bad-luck female you are. Animal Dan is no actor, I'm authentic. The movie called *Animal Dan's Domain* was the top box-office draw in 1981. Of course, when things began to fall apart it hurt show business and we didn't have any blockbusters after that. The books held out longer. In fact I think *Me and My Animals* might still be in print."

"Wildlife protection," said Gypsy, frowning as he remembered something from another century. "That's right, you and your wife took care of endangered and injured animals, raised them like your children."

"*I* did," said Animal Dan. "Neither one of my ninny wives ever gave a hoot. That's, I regret to admit, the only fakery in any of the books and films. Both of my unlucky wives loathed animals. Isn't that just like a woman? Marry a man known far and wide as Animal Dan and then complain about having a few animals around the place. My first wife wouldn't even let Taco into our bedroom at all."

"Who was Taco?" asked Annabelle.

Animal Dan snorted. "Only the most famous lion of modern times." He raised both gnarled hands, then let them drop. "What do they *learn* in school nowadays?"

Gypsy said, "If you've lived in this area for over fifty years, you must remember what things were like before the nation of Ngumi was set up."

"Better is how things were," answered Animal Dan. "When all these assorted tribes, and assorted nationals, decided to set up a democratic country things went from bad to worse. I tell you it's bicker, bicker, bicker and then have a coup. Bicker, bicker, bicker and another coup. Got so bad I have all my supplies delivered out here to Animal Dan's Domain. Last time I was into Capital

Town I walked right into three separate political assassinations, and I was only there for three-and-a-half hours." He shook his head, causing his beard to sweep his bare chest.

"Before," said Gypsy, "in the last century, you can tell me how things were?"

"Didn't I say I could? Don't start acting as half-witted as these two chums of yours." He put a hand on Gypsy's shoulder. "You come over to the main house, I'll tell you all about the old days."

"Did you ever hear of anyone named Dr. Hawksworth?"

The old man's eyes opened wider. "Dr. Hawksworth? Now there's a name I haven't heard in quite a spell," he said. "Yes, I knew her very well. Very well. Though if either of my dreadful wives were still extant, I'd have to deny it."

Annabelle held up the forlorn broom. "This won't do," she said.

"Do for what?" The big rattan chair creaked when Animal Dan swiveled to scowl at her.

She had emerged from the big dilapidated house to show them the nearly strawless broom. "Well, I really think someone ought to sweep out the dining room before we have dinner in there."

"No concern of yours," the old man said. "Nothing much wrong with it anyway."

"There's considerable debris," Annabelle informed him, "strewn about. Bones, scraps, quite a few objects I can't identify."

"Women always want to clean up, make everything

tidy," complained Animal Dan. "Can't convince them it's a not-very-tidy world. My second wife got so fussy I had to stop having the chimpanzees in for cards."

Shrugging, Annabelle tossed the broom back into the living room and came out to join them on the verandah.

Twilight was spreading across the plain, hiding the distant mountains, darkening the trees.

Gypsy was perched on the verandah railing. "I'd like to hear about Dr. Hawksworth."

"Used to be," said Animal Dan, "that visitors would get acquainted with my animals first. These days, there's no patience."

"I'd be bloody delighted to see your perishing animals." Walpole stood up on the step he'd been sitting on. "Wouldn't you, Annabelle?"

"No, I'd rather—"

"Sure you would, love. We'll go around back and peek into the blinking cages and pens and all. Let Gypsy and Animal Dan have a nice chat."

Annabelle said, finally, "Oh, okay."

When they were gone Gypsy repeated, "I'd like to hear about Dr. Hawksworth."

"Long time ago," began the old man, "not even in this century. I wasn't the ancient mariner you see now. When I stripped to the waist back then you didn't think you were looking at somebody's discarded leather valise. I was an exciting fellow when I was in my forties." He leaned his head back and folded his hands over his wrinkled stomach. "Only met her twice, but I can still remember. Lot of people, especially those ninnies who worked with her, thought Laura—that was her name—was a cold potato. Might even be some sort of dyke, they figured. Oh, but that wasn't true. I met her at a reception in the capital when there was no such country as Ngumi and the royalties from the books and movies

were pouring in. Laura was in government work, you know."

"I know."

The darkness moved in on the wooden porch.

"She was out here to set up a secret defense base, though that sure wasn't the story the U.S. Embassy was giving out," Animal Dan continued. "Laura never gave me any of that guff; she was always completely honest with me. They built this base underground, part of what they used to call . . . the ESO, I think. Back then nobody figured the world would go to pieces in the way it did." He paused, rubbing his rough old hands together. "Nothing ever goes wrong exactly the way you anticipate, except maybe a marriage."

"Did Laura Hawksworth ever talk to you about her work?"

"We talked about everything, didn't I tell you?" said Animal Dan. "Back then I was something, I could last all night. I never went in for guff and sweet talk between bouts, though. So we talked about more serious topics. I got to know a lot about what the United States of America was financing Laura to do."

It was night all around them now. Gypsy could hardly see the old man, but he listened to him. He learned a good deal about Dr. Hawksworth and the underground base in Ngumi. And he learned a few more things about himself.

TWENTY-ONE

A nightmare, rather than a memory.

The woman naked, lean. She drifted through the blackness, glowing faintly.

It was windy there, wherever he was. Gypsy could hear drapes flapping, windows rattling.

He tried to embrace her. He couldn't. His arms were strapped to his sides.

"Won't hurt," she whispered, her breath as harsh as the wind, swirling around his head. "Won't hurt, darling. Won't hurt."

Her face seemed to stay in darkness. Her body glowed, her hands were pulsing with light.

"Won't hurt, darling."

The fingers burned when they touched his head, made his skin smoke and spit. Both her hands clamped on his skull, burning.

Gypsy could feel the bones crumbling under the pressure.

The woman had ripped his head open, was scooping her burning fingers into it. They seized his brain, squeezed. Began tugging at it.

He screamed. Screamed to make her go away, to make this end.

He awoke. But only to another dream.

Laughter was struggling inside him. This was funny.

Funny because the surrounding day was so peaceful. So beautiful and quiet, the golden trees all around.

That was outside.

Inside it was noise, destruction. The flames roared, the walls burned, beams fell. Someone screamed until the fire took him and turned him black.

"This way! This way!"

Pulling him out of there, out into the sunlight and quiet.

Very hard to walk. What had happened?

It wasn't supposed to happen this way.

"Lie down, spread this on top of you."

Gypsy did that, got the dusty quilt over himself and huddled silently on the floor of the station wagon. It wasn't that uncomfortable; he could sleep.

Sleep brought dreams.

She held Gypsy's head clutched in her hand. That's all he was now, all that was left of him. A repulsive grey blob of something in the woman's grasp.

He wasn't even there.

Obviously not. He was across the room. Yes, he could see himself sitting in a chair.

But what was wrong with him? His arms dangled, his head hung sideways, his jaw was dropped open.

They put him in a suitcase, told him the show was over. Carried him off the stage while the audience applauded.

It was impossible to breathe in the dusty darkness; the screws at his joints ached. The shellac on his face was burning his cheeks.

"Don't thrash around so, someone might notice you."

The station wagon bounced and bounced, the road was terrible. Each bounce sent pain through Gypsy.

It was starting then. He was to wander, to search . . .

No, that wasn't what she had promised.

Something had gone wrong.

She'd named him Gypsy, yes. That was . . .

A joke?

There was little kindness in her, no humor. Her jokes were not to amuse but to hurt.

Gypsy was his name because she'd worked out a series of . . .

Of what?

He had to play it through to the end. Play what?

Then when it was over . . .

When it was over . . .

Sunlight.

Warm sunlight touching his face, Annabelle standing beside his bed. "You were shouting," she said, sitting on the edge. "I came in from my room."

"Sorry, I didn't mean to," he said, rising up. "Did I wake Walpole, too?"

"He was dead to the world when I passed his room, and Animal Dan is already outside with his animals," the girl said. "Could be I'm better tuned to your frequency."

Gypsy moved his hand to meet the one she was moving toward his arm. "Better go back to your room." He lowered the hand to the bed, let go.

"Can't anyone show concern for you?"

"Annabelle, I . . ." He hesitated, shaking his head. "I've learned something . . . something important. Not *all* of the pieces, but fairly soon, hopefully in Ngumi, I'll confirm what I suspect."

"That doesn't mean—"

"Yes, it does. I don't want to believe some of the things I suspect. In a way it's almost as though I can't. There's some kind of block inside me against accepting—"

"Walpole's been telling you things," the girl said. "But maybe he misunderstood what he'd read. You can't let what—"

"Not only Walpole. More and more lately I've been remembering. The dreams I've been having—"

"Dreams aren't noted for being historically accurate," Annabelle said. "You mustn't let a nightmare scare you."

Gypsy said, "Okay, it could be what's starting to surface is all cockeyed. As I say, sometimes I'm certain it's not true, other times . . . I wake up screaming."

"Maybe that's because you wake up alone," she said quietly.

Gypsy took her hand again.

"Not yet, Annabelle," he said.

She stroked his hand, stood, and left his room.

"Probably never," Gypsy said when the door had shut.

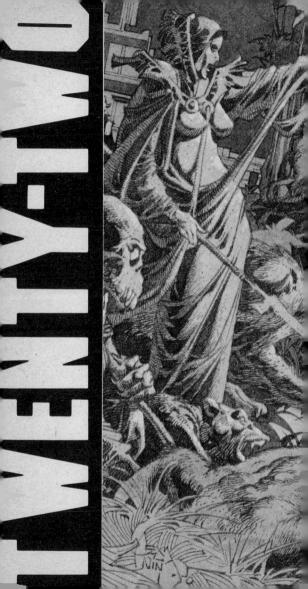

It had once been an airport, and there was still enough field space for the grey aircraft to take off from.

Jackita Teal guided the ship down the runway between the jagged ruts the Big Quake had left. The craft took to the air, swiftly climbing above the thin fog. "Next stop, Africa," she said.

Bookings was sagging in the passenger seat, breathing through his mouth and dabbing at his fat face. "The time is not right," he said.

"But it is, Pres," said the Scavenger leader.

"I know what we'll find there," said the perspiring man. "Trouble and despair."

The Scavenger ship was high above San Francisco, heading for the African continent.

"We've learned things, our agents in Ngumi," said Jackita. "Don't you realize we can use what was found to capture Gypsy, to nullify him temporarily?"

"If they can adapt it to our purposes in time."

"They can," she assured him. "When we set down at our little clandestine field near Ngumi we'll be very close to having Gypsy, a docile Gypsy."

"That's a word I'm reluctant to apply to him."

"Haven't you already agreed to using one of our new disablers on him?"

"I said I *might*," corrected Bookings, frowning out at blue sky.

"If we used what they found in the old ESO facility in Ngumi along with our brand-new disabler, there would be no problem." The gaunt woman scratched her cheek. "Granted, the disabler *alone* could fail. I think the surprise and shock we'd be adding will insure our success."

"We could accomplish all we want to accomplish in this sorry world without ever recruiting Gypsy to our side."

"Perhaps," admitted Jackita. "However, I want to

have him in our camp. Given his nature, he'd oppose us in everything we intend."

"That might add a little spice to things," said Bookings. "Some of our contests lately have been boringly easy to win."

"I'm willing to put up with some boredom."

Bookings unfurled his handkerchief. He slouched down in the passenger seat, draping the cloth over his pudgy face. "Awaken me when we reach the 'Dark Continent,' " he said.

TWENTY-THREE

Zebras came galloping through the twilight.

Gypsy pulled his two companions off the trail. The frightened striped animals passed by; dust and silence settled on the veld.

"Really got the wind up, those critters," observed Walpole as he returned to the trail.

Up ahead, roosting birds were scattering up out of the thin, flat-top trees.

"Something's frightening them," said Annabelle.

Gypsy nodded. "Ahead there."

Lights were coming on, brass band music came piping out of loudspeakers. A quarter of a mile ahead three huge landvans had parked beside a waterhole. One of them, the van with the most lights decorating it and the loudest music pouring forth, was tilted far to the right. Its front wheels had hit soft, mucky ground and it was sinking.

"As good a time, dear hearts, as any to learn the dignity of labor. Shoulders to the wheel, shove away!" a nasal voice was shouting. "Shoulder, Mkufu. That's your *buttocks*. Shoulder, here."

"This is no soft job, boss, like you promised."

"I didn't, bless your heart, expect the damned headquarters van to become mired. Heave now, lads, heave. That's your *elbow*, Mkufu."

"Appears you're stuck in the mud, old chap." Walpole stopped to watch the half-dozen struggling men.

"Very astute you are, young fellow. Exactly the type I'm looking for." Overseeing the Black and White men who were trying to extricate the heavy van was a short man in a two-piece white playsuit. He wore a white pith helmet on his slightly oversize head, a red flower in his lapel. "I can place you immediately in a loving home."

"Who'd do the loving?"

"Your employers, obviously. I am Captain Oxbow." He indicated the illuminated sign on the side of the stuck

van and read it aloud to Walpole: *Captain Oxbow's Job-mobile. Headquarters Of The Famous VOLUNTEER SLAVES OF THE WORLD! I Have A Job For YOU!*

"Don't much fancy that *slave* part," Walpole informed the white-suited man.

"You must put the emphasis on the word *volunteer*, dear heart." There were two golden rings, thick with stones, on the hand he used now to tug at his ear. "We all know slavery is long gone, that slave traders have ceased to raid darkest Africa. The one thing, though, you had to say for slavery was that, despite some drawbacks, it provided security."

"Are you," Gypsy asked him, "going on into Ngumi?"

"Pleased to meet you, I'm Captain Oxbow." He held out his hand and waited until Gypsy shook it before continuing. "This spot, approximately five miles from the Ngumi border, is as close as we come. A very unsettled country is Ngumi, especially in Capital Town. Mkufu, let's see a little more enthusiasm in the pushing department before the van sinks on us."

"Signed up to be a household servant, boss, not a human towtruck. My contract with Volunteer Slaves clearly states—"

"We'll reexamine your contract when this van is on dry land once more, dear heart."

"Maybe I can help." Gypsy walked over to the straining, grunting men. He reached out an arm and pushed at the bright red front of the landvan.

The stuck wheel made a slurping, popping noise. The van rolled several yards until it rested completely on solid ground.

"Did you pay attention, Mkufu?" asked the captain, smirking and snorting. "*There's* the way to do it."

"Volunteer slaves have no need for superhuman powers, boss."

The captain hurried over to Gypsy. "I am prepared to offer you a splendid contract. Volunteer Slaves can place you in a job where you'll—"

"Not interested," said Gypsy. "I have to get on into Ngumi."

"What are you earning at your present trade? I bet it's some dead-end sort of job," said the captain. "You'll be drawing a nice fat pay envelope if you sign up with—"

"Nope. No, thanks." He resumed walking.

"What about you two?" Oxbow asked Annabelle and Walpole. "I can fill in a Servitude Agreement for the pair of you, place you as butler and cook in a very genteel home in a pleasant New England town called What's Left Village. Might involve a little woodchopping and snow shoveling at times, and possibly a tiny bit of guerilla repelling when the food raid season is on. All in all a dandy situation for—"

"We're with *him*, mate." Walpole tipped an imaginary hat, took hold of Annabelle's arm, and urged her along in the wake of Gypsy.

"Perhaps you'd prefer a situation as gamekeeper and governess in a pleasant English county known as Underground Sussex, where all you have to . . ."

The inn, which had no name, was built near high trees not more than half a mile from the Ngumi border. From its terrace you could see the explosions in Capital Town, hear the gunfire and even much of the shouting and screaming.

"It violates the bloody Three Musketeers nature of our relationship," Walpole was saying while slouched in a canvas chair. "I mean to say, gov, I was of the opinion we weren't going to separate anymore."

Gypsy was standing near the low stone wall around the terrace. "I want to get more of an idea what Capital Town's like," he told his two companions, "before we all go in there."

"You know what it's like." Annabelle, annoyed, left her chair at their outdoor dining table. "The people who run this place told you; so did old Animal Dan. It's violent, wild, dangerous. We expect that."

"Righto, gov. We ain't about to shirk."

Gypsy said, "I'm going in there alone first."

Walpole let his hands climb up as high as his shoulders, then let them sink into his lap. "Might as well have signed up with that Oxbow cove to become a gamekeeper for some perishing toff. I know I've stumbled into a few traps along the way, gov, but when it comes to a pure and simple riot or brawl I can—"

"We don't know exactly what's going to happen in Ngumi," cut in Gypsy. "From talking to Animal Dan I have a pretty fair idea of where the old ESO facility was and what may be there now in Capital Town. I also have the key I told you about earlier. I'm sure the two are connected. I don't know what sort of hazards I'll have to overcome, what sorts of moves the Scavengers may—"

"All the more reason to continue as a team," insisted the girl, approaching him. "The three of us can—"

"No, you wait here," Gypsy said. "I'll come back for you tomorrow."

"Suppose you don't?" Walpole stretched out of his chair. "Suppose the bloody Scavengers and the locals all gang up on you?"

"That's a possibility," admitted Gypsy.

"You don't think we'll sit here on our ruddy rumps a-waiting for you then, do you?"

"It would be better if you did," said Gypsy.

"Should you not be back by this time tomorrow, gov,

we'll be charging right into Capital Town after you," promised Walpole.

"Let's leave it at that." Gypsy turned and walked away from the inn and his friends.

He had been walking for nearly five minutes when he heard, over the mounting noise of the fracases in Ngumi, his name being called.

In among the trees on the right of the roadway, on a high twisted branch, sat the vulture. Its eyes glowed brightly in the darkness. "There's still time to throw in the old towel, Gyp."

"Don't think I will." He left the road and ventured in among the dark trees. "What do you know about Ngumi?"

"All there is to know," the hunched bird replied. "You ought to realize by now, palsy-walsy, I'm one step short of being a walking encyclopedia. *Flying* encyclopedia. Why not quit?"

"The game isn't over."

"Listen, Gypo," the vulture said in a voice close to a whisper, "this is going to be a dangerous one. So why don't you—"

"Dangerous how?" he asked. "You mean the challenge set up for me here fifty years ago is still operational?"

"There's that, yep. And more."

"Such as?"

"Ngumi's Capital Town is not the most tranquil place you could blunder into."

"I'm aware of that."

"The test all by itself is a ballbuster," continued the bird. "Dr. Hawksworth could really come up with some dandies. *You* know *that* from the tests you've already met. This new one's a pip. You think that little ride you had over Model Africa was something? Wait until you get to Ngumi."

"I'm prepared to face it. Anything else you have to tell me?"

"The Scavengers are going to . . . aw, why bother you with that? Since you're determined to go ahead with this, you might as well go in with an unclouded mind."

"You're hinting, in your deft way, the Scavengers have agents in Ngumi who know I'm coming?"

"Better even than agents, my lad."

"Meaning?"

"I'll let you find out that answer on your own. You can't expect me to do all the work. After all, it's your game." The vulture unfurled its large wings and went flapping up and away.

TWENTY-FOUR

The border station exploded.

Its roof, the curved red tiles moving further and further apart, went climbing up into the dark sky. Flames and sparks followed, whooshing and crackling upward.

Two Black men were crouched by the side of the road, their backs against a sturdy parked communications van.

"Station again?" one of them said, not looking in the direction of the recent blowup.

"Sounded like it, didn't it?"

"Do we want footage?"

"Probably not, it's going to look pretty much like the last two border guard cottage explosions."

"Last *three*."

"*Two*. The one before the last two had the flower boxes in the windows."

"That was four or five stations ago."

"No, it was . . ." said the other man, holding up his hand and ticking off his fingers, "one-two-three-four . . . you're right."

"Sure, because I remember all the flower petals scattering when the station went up. 'A kaleidoscope of natural beauty,' I commented, 'in the midst of death and blood.'"

"You got the Pulitzer-Mauldin Prize for that, didn't you?"

"No, that was for describing the girls' school conflagration."

"Oh, was . . . who are *you*?"

Gypsy had hit the dirt when the explosion rocked the night. He was now rising, dusting himself off, a few feet from the roadside newsmen. "A tourist," he replied.

"Nobody visits Ngumi for fun."

"Is there maybe an angle in this guy?" One of the newsmen got up. "I'm Bert Johnson, with RWBS." He was thin, small, about thirty-two.

"That stands for Remaining World Broadcasting System." His associate remained on the ground. "I'm Alistair Tempesta. Probably you've heard or seen my 'Behind The Violence' stuff on the network."

"Can't say I have."

"Maybe he comes from a country with no television or radio, Al."

"Where do you come from?"

"Elsewhere," said Gypsy. "I'll be getting—"

"Wait, wait," said Johnson. "I sense a news yarn here."

Tempesta was heavyset, slow-moving. He began to get up now. "You've been on the Ngumi beat too long, Bert. After all this violence, anybody calm who happens along looks like news to you. This guy's probably just another dullard with no news value at all."

"You're right," Gypsy said. "I am. Could you tell me how far I am from the Capital Town Sportsdome?"

Tempesta stood all the way up. "Come on, now. Nobody in his right mind would go near there. Not during the African Olympics."

"African Olympics?"

"It's like the Olympics," amplified Johnson, "only restricted to African athletes. Very controversial right now, and lots of the African nations are boycotting."

"Resulting in," added Tempesta, "only thirty-four African countries sending athletes."

"Black pro-Mzaha forces object to the games," said Johnson, "and are threatening a riot."

"White anti-Mzaha forces assert that pro-Mzaha forces are always threatening a riot and are giving the African Olympics their wholehearted support."

"Meanwhile pro-Mkalimanis in Capital Town are charging both pro- and anti-Mzaha people with anti-Ngumi sentiments."

"In a statement issued this morning General Mzaha's press secretary and gunmaster flailed the pro-Mkalimani faction, charging General Mkalimani with plotting a coup."

"Mkalimani, since he's always plotting a coup, didn't deny this. His public relations director and boxing coach announced later in the day—"

"Very illuminating," said Gypsy. "I should listen to you two more often. How far is it to the Sportsdome?"

"Six miles straight ahead." Johnson drew a ballmike out of his pocket. "I'd still like to interview—"

"Thanks, but I can't." Gypsy resumed his hike.

"Hey, wait," called Johnson.

Tempesta put a restraining hand on his colleague's arm. "No story there, Bert," he told him. "That guy isn't news."

Whump!

Preston Bookings ducked. "Can't we blank the ceiling, draw curtains, do something?"

"It's only paint," said Jackita Teal. She was reclining on a nineteenth-century sofa.

Bookings scowled up at the plyodome over the living room area. "An entire bucket of paint. Dreadful color as well. Ocher." He watched the latest flung bucket's contents spilling and slurping across the curved dome. "It's disgusting when the different colors start to mingle. Ocher and vermilion and brindle. Ugh."

"You're starting to sound like Rolfe."

"What's that meant to imply?" He tugged out his handkerchief and patted his cheeks. "Don't try to undermine my masculinity. That's one thing I have no doubts about. Why'd you say that anyway?"

Jackita laughed.

Bookings sucked at his teeth and walked angrily around the circular room before dropping into a bentwood rocker. "We didn't have to come to Ngumi," he said, "risking life and limb, taking a chance of having bodily harm done to us."

Wham!

He bobbed out of the rocker.

"They've shifted to dynamite," observed Jackita.

"How can Rolfe stand it here? The neighbors obviously hate him."

The Scavenger leader shook her head. "It's not him; they have nothing against Rolfe at all," she said. "But in that hotel over there there's a bunch of pro-Mkalimani people, and the guest house on the other side of us shelters some anti-Mkalimani people. When they take to throwing things at each other Rolfe is simply in the middle. No need to worry, Pres, the dome can withstand—"

Whammo! Kachunk! Bum!

"Now they're throwing *people*," cried Bookings.

A White man in a striped one-piece fightsuit had landed, backside down, on the left slant of the plastic roof dome and was slowly sliding down it. Smeared with paint, he gave one disgruntled yell before slipping off into the two stories of darkness between this house and the next.

"No doubt," said Jackita, "he accidentally fell from a balcony over there while trying to fling something."

"What a country," said Bookings, "what a world."

"We'll remedy some of that."

"Sometimes I have doubts. So much violence, so much arguing, so much just plain—"

Dringg! Ring!

"Don't jump, it's okey-doke. Only me, gang. Hi." A slim Black man had come into the room through a panel in the flooring.

"What's that dreadful ringing?"

"Alarm system. On the blink a little, got paint in it, I think," said Rolfe Nyoka. "Pres, you're looking awful mad."

"Annoyed," corrected the fat man. "I'm annoyed with all this noise and violence."

Rolfe giggled. "You ought to be over at the Sportsdome. Gosh, it's really wild over there." He settled down on the Persian rug. "One of the factions is burning bleachers. Did you ever smell plastic burning? P.U."

Jackita asked, "Were you successful?"

The Black man stretched full out on the rug, studying the plastic ceiling. "You know, that paint makes some swell effects, makes the stars look very cute." He locked his hands behind his head. "Yes, I was successful, Jackie. I always am."

"Vanity, vanity," muttered Bookings. "It probably won't work."

"Golly, don't go picking on me because you're annoyed with the factions, Pres. Everything's going to work fine."

Jackita said, "You found it?"

"Right where the doctor's papers indicated," Rolfe answered. "*Still*, to anticipate your next question: *in working order*. I was able to make your suggested changes with no trouble. And I planted the other stuff. Gosh, I bet it really surprises your pal Gypsy."

"What else," asked the gaunt woman, "remains down there?"

"All kinds of things." Rolfe sat up and hugged his knees. "Seems like Dr. Hawksworth had herself a little apartment. She kept another diary there. Some of it's about affairs she had with people like animal trainers and such, but there's quite a good part devoted to your pal."

Bookings came puffing over to him. "Where is this diary? Didn't you have the sense to bring it to us?"

"You really look fat from this angle, Pres," said Rolfe. "Relax now. I left the book there so Gypsy could find it. More bait for the trap."

"Very good," said Jackita.

"Good?" interjected Bookings. "What's good about it? We may—"

"Everything will work out," said Jackita.

Rolfe giggled once again. "Gosh, yes," he said.

TWENTY-FIVE

"The next event will be . . . the next event will be . . . good heavens!"

Kaboom!

Blam!

The glow of the explosions illuminated the Sportsdome. A rich orange color pressed against the curved plaz panels.

A block away from the arena when the explosions shook the place, Gypsy broke into a run.

"Remain in your seats! Remain in your seats, don't panic!" urged the unsteady voice coming out of all the loudspeakers which dotted the dome. "Play the national anthem to calm . . . I don't know . . . any one of the national anthems. No need to stampede, ladies and gentlemen."

At the first entrance that Gypsy came to the ticket taker was dead. A redhaired boy, flat on his back, part of his chest blown away. A swirl of ticket stubs fanned out across the tiles from his dead fingers.

Gypsy went through the arched entryway the boy had been guarding.

"Down this way! They ran down this way!"

"Which faction?"

"Anti-Mzaha."

"That's the side I'm on, swine!"

Bam!

Zam!

Two security guards were shooting it out in the tubular green corridor.

Gypsy avoided getting hit himself and continued on.

"Let me go!"

Around the next curve a White girl was struggling with two husky White guerillas in one-piece yellow fightsuits.

"This is part of war, miss."

"Yeah, they call it rapine or something."

"Let me go, dammit."

"Off!" advised Gypsy. He paused long enough to throw the two assaulters into the wall.

"Thanks," said the girl. "Every time there's a coup around here, it gets crazy. In Ngumi there's a coup about every . . . wow!"

The walls shuddered, groaned. The ceiling buckled.

The girl took hold of Gypsy, arms tightening around his ribs. "Lots of explosives going off upstairs," she said.

"Is this likely to keep going on?"

"Afraid so. This feels like it's going to be a full-scale ruckus—might wreck the whole dome."

"And what's underneath."

"How's that?"

"Better do what I have to do right now tonight," he decided, pushing the girl gently away from him. "Will you be able to get away from here safely?"

"Aren't you coming?"

"Something to do down below."

"Nothing below but lockers and such."

Gypsy hurried away.

"Thanks!" the girl called after him.

The explosions, duller now, were becoming more frequent. Gypsy worked his way through the heating plant beneath the locker rooms of the arena. Animal Dan had been right: this part of the structure was older than the aboveground building. It had been here when the earlier buildings had concealed the ESO facility. If the old man's memory continued to be reliable, there should be a panel immediately next to this row of ducts.

"Yes, here it is." Gypsy had a feeling some memory of his own was also guiding him to the spot. He ran his fingertips over the section of metallic wall and located the very slight depression near the floor.

The panel quivered and hummed before it slowly slid open. Light blossomed, dim and fuzzed, and a smell of aged dust came drifting out at Gypsy.

Without hesitating, he stepped through the wall. Light strips ran in three parallel rows along the low metal ceiling of the down-slanting corridor. Designed to be activated by the opening of the panel, many of them no longer produced any light.

"Lots of things can die in fifty years," Gypsy said to himself.

The tunnel dug deeper and deeper into the ground.

He came eventually to another panel, pressed it, and stepped through the opening into a large square room. Only one of the lightstrips in here functioned, making a stripe of illumination across the middle of the office.

Trusting to Animal Dan's recollection of his rendezvous with Laura Hawksworth, Gypsy opened the middle door of the three in the far wall. He was on guard as he stepped into a new corridor, watchful for whatever might have been left here to test him.

But there was nothing. He traveled the pale blue corridor safely, reached the seventh door, a yellow one, and twisted its handle. A small whirr issued from within and Gypsy tensed. Scanning the door area, he noticed a small hole far up the jamb. Letting go the door, Gypsy extracted the rod he had found at the other Ngumi and tried it in the hole. It fit perfectly; something within the wall made a turning-off click. Whatever safety trap had awaited him was deactivated now.

This was the door to the rooms Dr. Hawksworth had used as living quarters when she visited this particular installation. A very faint scent still lingered in the room. The lightstrips in here had been fashioned into table lamps, three of them, and each glowed softly after he touched the light button beside the entryway.

A parlor office, furnished in the style of the last century. A large desk, made of real wood, sat diagonally in one corner. He approached it.

Dust had settled on everything. Papers and folders still rested on the green blotter. Right on top of everything, held down by a chunk of cloudy amber, was a note—addressed to him.

Gypsy, it said in neat faded printing, *the next stop is Rio.*

Somewhat gingerly, Gypsy took up the note. This wasn't a plant of the vulture's. The paper was old, yellowed, and crisp, the ink very pale. This note had been left for him fifty years ago. Left by Dr. Hawksworth probably, who'd never been able to come back here.

"This was part of the game, then." Carefully folding the old sheet of notepaper, Gypsy thrust it into a pocket.

Next in the dusty pile was a file folder labeled *Gypsy*. He pulled back the desk chair, sat down, and opened it. After a glance behind him, he turned his attention to the contents of the folder.

"Doesn't make much sense," he said, frowning.

There were only a few newspaper clippings—very old, in worse shape than the note, edges curled and crumbling. There were seven clippings in all. Large ones, front-page stories with enormous bold headlines. *Kenner Killed. Assassin Vanishes.*

The whole collection dealt with this incident which had taken place a half-century ago in the United States. The official's name had been Elias Kenner, the assassin a young man named Brian Jepson.

"Don't Believe He Could Have Done It" Asserts Assassin's Best Friend.

New Haven, Ct. In his office at Fairfield Academy

*Associate Professor Douglas Demby today insisted that
his close friend Brian Jepson, the alleged assassin, cannot
possibly have committed the crime.*

*"Yes, I know it was on television," admits Demby,
who teaches 19th Century Literature at this prestigious
institution, "I saw the d—— broadcast myself. I saw
Brian shoot him. I saw it all live, but I don't believe it. He
simply wasn't that kind of man."*

*Demby hasn't seen his longtime friend for almost a
year, and he acknowledges the possibility Jepson might
have suffered some kind of . . .*

Gypsy let the clipping drop back to the packet. His
eyes nearly shut, he strained to remember. Kenner must
have been in government when . . . back when he'd gone
to sleep, fallen into his half-century coma or whatever it
was. So he ought to remember the man. But he didn't. It
was almost as though he couldn't.

He picked up the clipping again, studied the blurry
photo of young Brian Jepson. Familiar, that face, that
quirky smile. The name—he had heard before. This was
someone who might have been a friend of his, someone
who knew him.

"Lot of good that does," Gypsy said.

According to these ancient newspaper stories, Jepson
had vanished. *National Security Office Denies
Knowledge Of Assassin's Whereabouts.* But apparently
there had been a strong suspicion the government had
grabbed Jepson immediately.

Gypsy rubbed at his forehead. The incidents these brit-
tle fragments were recounting sounded very familiar. "Of
course they are—it was a major story," he said. "Anyone
who was alive then would be familiar with these events."

And yet . . .

No use, the thought eluded him.

He pushed backed slightly from the doctor's desk. On

a corner rested a black, leather-bound journal.

Gypsy opened it at random.

. . . Emerson much too sentimental. He professes to be arguing chiefly on the grounds of efficiency, says there is absolutely no need for it. I think differently. I intend to go ahead, and I have both the blessing of the US Clandestine Research Office and ESO. We'll build more, no matter what protest Dr. Emerson comes . . .

He turned several pages.

. . . opportunity. Though the amount of string-pulling and cajoling has been incredible. Thank God I was on the spot when it happened. Otherwise there's no telling what NSO would have done with him. With what was left of him. Emerson tells me I'm behaving like a mad scientist in a cheap movie. He could well be right, but we're going to go ahead with this. The possibilities are fascinating, and I'm incredibly anxious to pit the two types of androids against each other. Once the work is completed I—

"Hello, Gypsy."

He hadn't sensed it at all. He looked up from Dr. Hawksworth's journal to see a figure standing quite close to the desk.

It was himself.

TWENTY-SIX

Jackita Teal pressed her hands tightly together, the fingertips growing red. The viewscreen on the marble-top table pulled her toward it. She sat hunched, very close to it, breathing very slowly and carefully.

"No one else can see anything with you right on top of that thing," complained Bookings.

The Scavenger leader didn't move. "Quiet—and listen."

"Boy, I sure planted that bugcamera good," remarked Rolfe. "That's a nice, clear, sharp picture, all right. I've always been good with technical things, ever since—"

"Quiet, quiet." The gaunt woman's shoulders narrowed; she tilted even closer.

On the screen they saw Gypsy twice.

Rolfe said, "Golly, she did excellent work."

Jackita's hand flashed out to twist the volume dial on their monitoring device. "The tests she'd planned for him here wouldn't work unless the replica was exact."

"We're not to have more violence, then?" Bookings inquired.

"Not from them. Everything left for Gypsy in that room was intended as a challenge to the stability of his identity. Those clippings we saw him leafing through, the journal, and now this marvelous android duplicate."

". . . know anything?" Gypsy was asking the replica of himself.

"I know I'm to confront you, to greet you," replied the android. "To observe, to check your reactions to me."

"But that was the task set for you a full half-century ago. In all that time—"

"You must be wrong. No time has passed," the duplicate told him. "It was only hours ago I was stationed in the concealed alcove, instructed to—"

Boom!

Kaboom!

The image on the screen shook.

"Darn those guys at the arena," said Rolfe. "They're going to destroy the whole place."

"We should have, as I suggested, taken—"

"Shush, both of you, so I can hear."

"Hear? They're setting off bombs practically on top of that underground facility and you criticize me for—"

"Quiet, be quiet."

Gypsy stood close to the android duplicate. "Everything went wrong," he said. "Everyone involved with this project is probably long since dead."

"Not you."

"No, not me. I've come here to find out why."

Rolfe said, "He'll deviate from his original program about here. Thanks to my modifications."

"Fifty years," the android said, "is a time span I find it difficult to—"

Blam!

Bang!

Kaboom!

One of the lamps jumped from its table in that underground room. A crack appeared in the metal ceiling and began growing.

"This whole place is in danger." Gypsy grabbed the duplicate's arm. "We'll get out and—"

"Can't do that. Not part of my duties." From a pocket he removed a small silver rod. "Have to use this on you."

"The disabler!" breathed the watching Jackita.

"We almost have him," said Rolfe, giggling.

Gypsy's hand pushed against the android's chest.

"Have to use this on you." The duplicate was thrown off balance; it went staggering toward the wall.

Bam!

Kawham!

The ceiling of the underground office burst, hunks of metal, shards of plastic, wires all began to pour down.

The watching Scavengers saw a thin beam leap from the end of the rod and go sizzling in Gypsy's direction.

The picture died.

Jackita twisted all the dials.

The screen stayed black.

Rolfe said, "Those crazy factionalists have ruined everything."

The woman ran to the exit panel in the floor. "We've got to get over there and dig him out."

"You're inviting death," said Bookings, who had not moved.

"Nonsense. I've enough weapons and gadgets to assure—"

"Go easy, Jackie," warned Rolfe. "We maybe have a full-scale revolution in the works in Capital Town. Wisest thing is to get out of the country, right away."

"No." She lifted the panel.

". . . Bert Johnson has that story."

"This is Bert Johnson in Capital Town, Ngumi . . . or rather I'm on the outskirts of Ngumi myself while our courageous flying robot cameras are at the scene of this newest outbreak of violence . . . it's not an outbreak, exactly, since they're always fighting about something in Ngumi. Tonight, however, only scant minutes ago . . . well, about an hour-and-a-half, actually . . . at any rate, intense rioting broke out at the African Olympics. You can see on your screen that the Sportsdome . . . it's not really even a dome anymore, is it? The damage has been estimated at—"

"Blimey!" Walpole sat up on his bed. He'd dozed off while watching a folksong discussion. He awoke to see the smoldering ruins of the sports arena. "That's where the gov was going to nose around, ain't it?"

Jumping off the bed, where he'd been dozing fully clothed, the lanky young man dashed over to the small battered television set his room at the inn was provided with. "What about the blooming casualties, mate?" He slapped the side of the box a few times.

". . . possibly precipitated by some argument over the outcome of one of the athletic events. We'll be getting something on the causes of this violent outbreak from Alistair Tempesta shortly. An interesting sidelight to the series of massive explosions which shook the arena is that they revealed a considerable underground structure. Spokesmen for the Sportsdome maintain they had no prior knowledge of any—"

"That's the bloody place Gypsy had to get to," said Walpole. "Did he go there tonight to case the setup? Coo, why didn't I insist on tagging along?"

Spinning on one booted foot, Walpole headed for the door.

It opened before he reached it. Annabelle stood on the threshold, buttoning her shirt. "You've heard?"

"About the perishing explosions in the Sportsdome? I bloody well have."

"Gypsy was probably there."

"My feelings, exactly."

"They haven't said anything about finding any body in the underground part of it."

"They haven't said anything about anything."

"Apparently," the girl said, "there's considerable

fighting all over the town."

"Even so," said Walpole, "we got to find the gov. I mean to say, he might be trapped down under there. Buried in rubble and debris, as it were."

"I don't think . . ." The girl reached out all at once to grip his arm.

"What's wrong, lass?"

"Nothing, I guess." She shook her head. "Gypsy is the one who can see into the future sometimes—not me."

"Did you go and have some kind of blooming vision?"

"No, not really," she said. "More just a feeling, an awful feeling that sort of took hold of me for a moment."

"About what?"

"I suddenly had the terrible notion that we're never going to see Gypsy again," Annabelle said.

TWENTY-SEVEN

Daybreak.

The night went away.

Brightness came sweeping through the wooded area where he was lying. Face down, he grimaced, sniffing. A strong smell of smoke surrounded him.

He pushed at the ground with his hands. Pushed until he had managed to lift himself to his knees.

Grass and brown earth beneath him. Nothing burned or burning.

He saw his hands. They were smeared with soot.

So were his clothes.

He rubbed his fingertips across his face; they came away blackened.

What had happened?

He struggled, stood up. He started to fall, had to catch hold of the trunk of a tree and hug it to keep himself from falling down.

He turned his head suddenly.

"Thought I . . . heard something."

Nothing. A few birds chattering, getting ready for the new day. Nothing else.

What he was hearing was inside his head.

Voices shouting. Explosions. One after another. Explosions.

And something else.

Himself. He was staring at himself. Talking to himself in . . . where had that been?

A house someplace. No, an office.

Right. An office and staring at himself.

In a mirror, obviously.

No, but it wasn't. The other self had . . . a gun? Something in his hand. Something which hurt him.

Not as badly as they'd expected. But . . .

That didn't explain the fire and the explosions.

He couldn't explain them.

For that matter he couldn't explain how he'd come to this wood. Come from . . . where?

Where had he been? He was standing in a room . . . an office . . . facing himself . . . and there was the weapon and it hurt him. Then everything was collapsing.

That was it. Everything had collapsed, fallen in on him.

He'd . . . what had he done? Dug his way out.

He examined his hands again, noticing the fingers were bruised, bloody.

So he'd dug himself out of . . . out of wherever that had been.

Fighting.

Yes, there'd been people. Hundreds of them. Hundreds of people fighting.

They'd chased him and . . . no, that wasn't right. That memory was from someplace else, some other time than now.

He'd gotten through the fighting crowds, fought his way through. Come this way because . . .

Someone he had to meet. Last night. This morning. Had to meet them . . . that's right. More than *one* someone. Had to meet *them* . . . where?

No answer. Nothing inside his head to tell him.

He'd come this far. Last night, it must have been. After . . . after whatever it was had happened.

He had made it this far and fallen. Slept. Now it was morning and he was supposed to . . .

Another blank.

Meet someone, go somewhere.

Better walk awhile. Might clear his head so—

"Well, good morning. What a pleasant surprise."

A short man in a brilliant white suit was coming through the woods toward him. The sun sliced down through the branches, making the rings on his extended

hand sparkle and gleam.

Was this the man he was supposed to meet?

"Good morning," he replied. "I'm a little . . . confused. There's been . . . some kind of accident."

"So I can see, dear heart," said the white-suited man. "But surely you remember me? It's Captain Oxbow you see before you."

"Captain Oxbow? Yes . . . I guess I do know you . . . I met . . . met you when?"

"Why, we're old friends." Oxbow came close enough to pat him on the shoulder. "In fact, you were thinking about signing a contract with me."

"Contract?"

"For a job, for a splendid job to be provided by my organization," the captain explained. "Why, from the moment I saw you get that mired van of mine out of the muck and back on the straight and narrow, I knew I had to sign you up. Ah, yes, I've many many clients who'll be overjoyed at the opportunity of employing the likes of you, dear heart."

"I need a job," he asked, "do you think?"

"That you do. Come along back to my headquarters van, which is parked conveniently nearby. We'll draw up the necessary papers, we'll get you cleaned up and properly fed. What say?"

"I suppose . . . yes, I better come with you. Since we're friends."

"We are, we are!" the smiling Captain Oxbow assured him. "Friends, and now business associates." He started him walking in the direction of the van. "By the way, I don't believe you've ever told me your name."

"My name?" He frowned. "My name is . . . Brian Jepson."

"Come along with me then, Brian."

Sitting on a branch of a tree was the vulture. It had

been far enough from the meeting place to have gone un-noticed. It had been able to see and hear everything.

As the two men departed, it sat silently watching. There was a burning glow in the eye of the vulture.

FOR LOVERS OF THE COMICS—NOSTALGIC HUMOR WITH A THREE FOOT SLEUTH!

SCHLOMO RAVEN—IN FULL COLOR.
SEE PAGE FOUR.

WEIRD HEROES 6

NEW FANTASY AND SF BY FARMER, COVER, GOULART, REESE, NINO AND MORE!

FOR ORDERING INFORMATION
SEE PAGE FOUR.

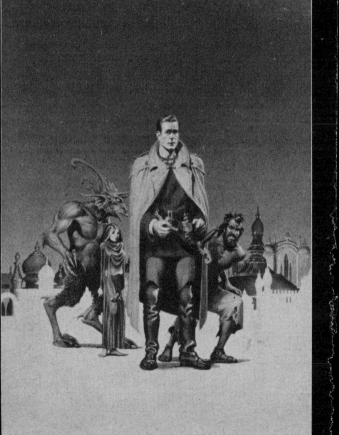

PHILIP JOSE FARMER
ROBESON

MICHAEL MOORCOCK
SEWARD

J. MICHAEL REAVES
KAMUS

BENJAMIN BOVA
ORION 2

With art by Howard V. Chaykin,
Alfredo P. Alcala, Stephen
Hickman and P. Craig Russell.
Edited and developed by
Byron Preiss. Available Nov. '77

ABOUT THE CONTRIBUTORS

Goulart on Goulart . . .

Despite my apparent youth, I've been writing professionally for about a quarter of a century. In that span of years something like two hundred of my stories and articles have appeared, in magazines ranging from *Playboy* and *Penthouse* to *Ellery Queen* and *Fantasy & Science Fiction*. I didn't get around to novels until 1968, when I wrote *The Sword Swallower*, but since then I've turned out about seventy five of the things. Over half of the novels have appeared under my own name, the rest using an assortment of pennames. Some multi-name authors have worked out elaborate biographies for their alter egos. All I know about mine is that they are even more crass than I am.

I was born in 1933, came East in the late 60s. I'm a native Californian and someone told me recently I have a California accent. Until then I assumed my style of speaking was an amalgam put together from imitating the announcers on boyhood radio serials and listening to my Portuguese relatives talking English. I attended the University of California at Berkeley, where I distinguished myself in ways other than academic. A week before I was set to commence graduate school, a San Francisco advertising agency offered me a job. I took it. From the ad game I learned how to drink three martinis at lunch and still find my way back to the office, how to sleep comfortably on top of an average size desk and how to write concisely. I gave up drinking and desktop naps some years ago, but I still suffer from that conciseness training. Which is why my novels are always a few pages shorter than anyone else's.

My wife, whom I married in 1964, is also a former advertising copywriter turned book author. Though she's a lot less concise than I am. We have two sons and live in Connecticut, where we almost pass for normal everyday commuters.

Most of my future writing plans consist of different ways to write less while earning more. I also have my eye on a Nobel Prize for literature, but they hardly ever seem to give that to a humorist.

Editor Byron Preiss . . .

Byron Preiss is a native of Brooklyn, New York. He holds a BA in liberal arts from the University of Pennsylvania and an MA in communications from Stanford University.

He has produced educational and leisure material for the Children's Television Workshop, Sesame Street and The Electric Company; The Model Cities Program, National Periodical Publications, Marvel Comics, and ABC Television, San Francisco.

Byron Preiss Visual Publications, Inc. specializes in the production of illustrated educational and fantasy material. It is involved with the production of two graphic series in conjunction with Harcourt Brace Jovanovich, *Weird Heroes* and *Fiction Illustrated*. The latter is America's first graphic novel revue; a sophisticated quarterly series of books produced in the visual storytelling format. Titles—mentioned elsewhere in this book—range from period humor to science fiction. Preiss has written three of the four initial volumes, including *Son of Sherlock Holmes*, a collaboration with artist Ralph Reese. Recently, the series were voted a Special Recognition by Comic Media readers in England.

Illustrator Alex Nino . . .

Alex Nino is aptly described by the phrase "an artist's artist." Respected by his fellow fantasy and science fiction artists as a versatile, innovative illustrator, Nino has spent his 16-year career blazing new paths in design and illustration. His compositions for various comic companies are among the most sensational in a field too burdened by repetition. A native Phillipino, Alex's first ten years as a professional were spent working exclusively for publications of that country. Of this work, friend and critic Orvi Jundis writes, "His graphic novel, *Gruaga, the Fifth Corner of the World*, is one of the highlights of fantasy art. . . . He has probably more drawing styles than anyone else in the field."

In 1970, Alex began working for American publishing companies, including National and Marvel Comics. This work added an entirely new coterie of fans to the Nino stable and established for him an international reputation as an illustrator of fantasy themes. In 1974 he won an award at the World Science Fiction Convention in Washington, D.C.